WING WALKING

WING WALKING

Don Meredith

Texas Review **Press**
Huntsville, TX

FIRST EDITION, 2000

Requests for permission to reproduce material from this work should be sent to:

Permissions
Texas Review Press
English Department
Sam Houston State University
Huntsville, TX 77341-2146

Acknowledgments

My first thanks are to Paul Ruffin for his encouragement and support over nearly twenty years. And thanks also to Phillip Parotti, George Garrett, and Gorman Beauchamp.

The author gratefully acknowledges financial assistance from the National Endowment for the Arts.

Portions of this work originally appeared, in somewhat different form, in *Home Movies* (New York: Avon Books, 1982), *Morning Line* (New York: Avon Books, 1980), *Folio*, *The Greensboro Review*, *Kingfisher*, *The Short Story Review*, *Slipstream*, and *The Texas Review*.

Cover design by Kellye Sanford

Library of Congress Cataloging-in-Publication Data

Meredith, Don, 1938-
    Wing Walking / Don Meredith.-- 1st ed.
        p. cm.
    Contents: The recital -- Desert music --At the punishment cliff for women -- Ferry from Kabatas -- Funny valentine -- Wing Walking -- Wanamaker -- French letters --The closer.
    ISBN 1-881515-32-X
    1. United States--Social life and customs--20th century--Fiction. I. Title.

PS3563.E7358 W5 2000
813'.6--dc21   00-045140

4

For my wife, Josie, who perservered.

With love and gratitude.

Table of Contents

WING WALKING

THE RECITAL

Dennis Brain, a certifiable Limey crank, a genius, a hornplaying fool, once performed Leopold Mozart's D Minor Concerto on a garden hose. It was a unique achievement, both musically and mechanically, and even down where the Ouachita River meanders through the piney woods and the pumped-out oil wells of southern Arkansas, Zatha Monroe's eleven-year-old heart kindled when she heard of it. A skinny, redheaded kid in grade-school music class, she was nuts about transatlantic canoe paddlers, Gypsy bear trainers, and the sub rosa careers of Tempest Storm and Lily St. Cyr.

A shrill soprano with dimpled elbows and heaving bosoms, Miss Mona Perkins was the glee club and song flute chorus leader. Customarily introduced at church functions and recitals as "Smackover, Arkansas's Answer to Kate Smith," Miss Mona relished the comparison. Clutching her bosoms she bowed deeply, cracked her painted lips in a grim smile, then burst into a chorus or two of "God Bless America." She was a large, sensitive and patriotic soul. By the time she reached "Through the night with the light from above," tears inevitably tracked her makeup, moistening her snowy cleavage. If she were present, Zath would just as inevitably lead Smackover's younger generation in a frenzied outbreak of mock-hysterics.

But when Miss Mona switched on the classroom phonograph and played a recording of Mr. Brain performing Johann Nepomuk Hummel's Horn Concerto, using an honest-to-goodness horn, then explained that Brain had kept his conventional brass instruments functioning and in tune with the help of rubber bands, paper clips, clothespins, and his own very talented spit, Zath was enthralled. But the idea of this virtuoso playing on a rubber tube thrilled her most.

Once she'd pumped Miss Mona for details, Zath vowed to equal his oddball moment in musical history. First, she hand-lettered posters announcing the upcoming feat, tacked them to fences, poles, and buildings, then bagged 15 feet of her papa's 5/8-inch Amazon garden hose. In Mr. Brain's configuration, the tube was exactly 148 3/4 inches long, with two 5/16 inch holes, the first 9 3/4 inches and the second 3 inches from the open end. The mouthpiece receiver was a large, wooden sewing thread spool, one end of which was drilled to fit snugly over the end of the hose, and the other to hold a horn mouthpiece. Zath's was more or less the same, give or take a few inches.

She snagged the spool from her mama's sewing basket and spun off yards and yards of scarlet thread that blew into webs that hung for years among the hydrangea bushes on the shady side of the house. The mouthpiece, a Vincent Bach 3/4C for players with dental configurations that cause embouchure problems, came from snag-toothed Lanny Pollard's trumpet case, left unguarded in the band room during lunch hour and therefore fair game.

Zath hustled this coveted object home in the bosom of her pinafore and locked it away in the rosewood box with her bracelet charms, lipsticks, and vials of sweet and powerful scents, a pair of Gypsy pink sponge rubber falsies, eyelash curlers, combs, brushes, and compact mirrors, all shoplifted from the crumbum sundry counters at Diamond's Five-and-Dime.

On a Saturday morning in spring when the grass was green as anything, and the sourweed, mustard, and horseradish flowers varnished the vacant lots, she packed her equipment aboard an American Flyer wagon and trucked it down to the wide space beside Vignola's Corner Grocery. Now and then a car rattled past on Calion and across Kraft. Crazy Mr. Rainey, a propeller spinning wildly on the peak of his beanie, spaded his melon patch. You could smell horse manure and turned earth. Zath sat spread-kneed on an upturned washtub, snaked the poisonous green garden hose around her gleaming Mary Janes, and waited with a certain hauteur for her audience to arrive.

The day was warm and breezy. Gum wrappers and cellophane from old Luckies packs spiraled in the dust devils that danced around the grocery's loading dock where the Vignola kids hung out, lagging soda bottle caps. They gave up their game and came Indian file through the tall grass to see what Zath was up to. The smallest, Angelo, was pantless. Joey, the biggest, was making a brave attempt to be the first kid on his block to grow a Jerry Colonna mustache.

This wasn't exactly the audience Zath had in mind when she tacked up the posters, but it might turn out all right. Everyone knew Italians loved music.

"Are you settin' up a hospital or what?" Joey Vignola wanted to know. His hand-me-down trousers of pale green corduroy worn thin as a dollar were shrunk so tight they showed off his ankles and what Zath thought of as his physique. She wished he'd go away. She couldn't take her eyes off him.

"Go on home now, Joey Vignola. You hear?"

"No law against watching."

"Watching what?"

"Watching you play doctor."

"Who says I'm playing doctor?"

"What else you gonna do with that rubber tube except give somebody an enema?"

"That's nasty, Joey Vignola!" She blushed, clutched the hose, and drummed her shoes in the grass. "Your mama should wash your mouth out with soap."

Had fun-loving Dennis Brain, puffing away at Papa Mozart's perky concerto, been subjected to such indignities? It seemed unlikely his good humor could have survived. Rather than finishing the horn piece, he might have taken his carefully prepared garden hose and wrapped it around Joey Vignola's neck.

Joey poked out his tongue.

She responded in kind.

He had lively dark eyes, she noticed, black and hard as the arrowheads farmers turned up in loamy river bottoms. His gleaming black hair swept over a frayed collar. He slouched, hooked his thumbs into his belt loops, and nudged himself toward her fascinated gaze.

"I'm playing music, not doctor," she said. "Leopold Mozart. And if you're going to hang around talking dirty and acting smart, Joey Vignola, you'll just have to shut up and listen."

He spat expertly between his bare feet. "What kinda music is this Leopold stuff?"

"Classical. Now pay attention. Soon as everyone gets here I'll begin."

Laughter broke under Joey's fuzzed lip. Who else would show at this chicken feed, classical-Leopold sandlot affair? No one, that's who. But just in case, he shooed his kid brothers before him and slouched nearer to have a clear shot at things.

She felt his eyes on her, clapped her knees together and yanked down her skirt. These were calculated moves that lacked the deep-rooted embarrassment you might have witnessed if she'd made them moments before. She wasn't sure what it was but she'd learned something from the way Joey prowled and stroked his would-be mustache and let his bottle-cap-lagging fingers curl from his belt loops, to say nothing of the amused hankering gleam in his black eyes.

Had her stuck-up manner sparked his interest? She guessed so—along with a few other things she was just beginning to know she had. She wasn't stewing about sexual equality. She figured, from the moment she saw Joey Vignola's spineless toe-dance in her direction, she was born with all the advantages.

"I'm still waiting." A smile replaced his laughter. "When's it going to begin?"

Ever so slightly she eased her knees apart. Not too far but far enough. "You have something better to do?" She edged back her skirt and pointed one Mary Jane toward paradise.

Joey's eyes brightened. "Maybe I do and maybe I don't. First I want to see."

"You'll see."

"I know, soon as everybody shows. Only, ain't nobody else coming."

"That's where you're wrong, Mr. Know-it-all."

Always a plunger, Zath waved a hand toward a corner of the grocery where a "Drink Dr. Pepper" sign hung at an angle. A commanding gesture, singular and direct. The response might have been an accident, one of those freaks of serendipity, though it was just as likely an act of pure feminine will. Sunburned and uniformed, bearing the burden of their athletic preoccupations, a handful of Southside kids rounded the corner on their way to Little League and shuffled through the grass.

"Hey, Vignola, what's going on?" Davy Henderson hollered to Joey, but it was Zath he was watching. Once, in the back of Home Ec., using 12-ounce gloves and the Marquis of Queensberry Rules, she'd beaten him to the punch and flattened him.

From the wary look in his jumpy blue eyes, you could tell he hadn't forgotten.

"Music," said Joey. Confronted by this cross-town detachment of blond stalwarts, he drew in behind his small brothers and let his eyes go blank. "Leopold What-ziz-name. Classy stuff. Stick around and give a listen."

"Yeah, you gonna sing, Vignola? Tra-la-la. Hah-hah!" A bum shortstop with a baloney sense of humor, Davy always did the talking.

Joey cut him off. "Zath's playing," he said. "Soon as she's ready. She toots this classy stuff like nobody you ever heard."

"I never heard no one."

"That's what I mean, she's the best."

Zath lifted the Amazon coils and snaked them several times around her shoulders. She listened as Davy and Joey talked about her as if she were some distant glowing object in deep space. With a grimace she puckered her mouth and spat into Lanny Pollard's mouthpiece, then stretched her fingers over the holes Mr. Brain had prescribed—closed the first hole above middle D and both holes above D in the staff. She pressed the mouthpiece to her lips, breathed deeply, and raised her eyes for a final measurement.

The ball players pulled in close. Maybe they were onto something—a squeeze bunt up the third base line. Only Davy edged away, restless and cagey, as if he'd caught a sign and was looking for a sizzler to come licking across the infield. Put off by the ball hawks, Joey drifted back. He smiled, confident, cool as anything, his dark eyes filling with Zath's slightly parted knees, the pleasure he drew from the pressure of her lips on the brass cup.

She grasped the tube, met Joey's look and began to play, puffing gently at first, then harder, and finally with dizzying concentration.

From the first note, a quivering, toneless, feline cry, a dry wheel turning on the ungreased axle of disaster, she was stunned by her fantastic presumption. As far as the mechanics went, she hadn't a notion what she was doing. Sheet music, with its curious alphabet of staves and semiquavers, bars and breves, baffled her completely. Even if she had a faultless ear and perfect pitch, they'd have proved useless. She'd never heard the piece. What a knockdown! All along she believed the music would somehow take care of itself.

Davy wasn't fooled for a second. "What's this?" He was up and shouting. He waved his fat freckled hands in Zath's face. "You're a faker. This is nothing but noise. You couldn't boogie out of a wet paper bag!"

She ignored him and went on playing. Hadn't Papa Mozart and Dennis Brain and Miss Mona pulled up their socks and simply performed? It was the American way. She'd heard it a million times: You can do anything you put your mind to. So, sweating and puffing, thumping her Mary Janes in the dust, and tootling for all she was worth, she heard the music grow sweeter and believed she'd become a conduit from the spheres and was actually playing the concerto she had never heard.

Who can blame her for taking no notice of Davy Henderson's catcalls? It wasn't her lookout if he had a bad ear and worse manners. She knew she was playing like an angel. Obbligatos, pizzicatos, adagios, and sfozandos flowed from the old green garden hose as if Orpheus and the Muses were taking some licks.

Davy was so outraged you'd have thought he'd spent a month's allowance for the privilege of hearing Zath's exquisite hose music. He shouted, waved his arms, tossed pebbles into the tube's open end. His ball-playing buddies saw this as a sporting pursuit and waded in. As happens when the poetic runs afoul the intolerance of bozos, pebbles became stones, and the target shifted until Zath herself was peppered dangerously.

Martial escalation turned into a fight, a kids' brawl of taunts and dares, considerable shoving, a few punches, and a whole lot of dust. Zath stayed at the center, hollering and swinging what she could, while Joey hung back, weighing personal safety against uncertain promises. Finally, when one of the ball players had a grip on the famous garden hose and threatened to garrote poor Zath, and Joey's pantless kid brother Angelo had his teeth deep into Davy's ankle, Joey bounced in to take a whack at the would-be garroter. He missed, turned for another try, and caught a rock on the ear. Zath yanked the hose from her neck and flung the rock thrower to the ground. Joey plunged in, got off a pair of well-timed jabs, and was jerked back, his ear hot with pain. Davy was still trying to shake little Angelo from his leg.

Starry-eyed, Zath always insisted it was the force of Joey Vignola's frenzied longing that won the day. She was dreaming. It was Angelo's teeth and the possession of high technology. With the upturned washtub as a shield, Zath fended off the clods and stones winging her way while she twirled the hose in smart, whistling circles.

After Davy caught the force of the hose across his nose and retreated, bloodied and raving through the tall grass with his crew, Zath and the Vignola gang moved in triumph onto the shaded loading dock.

Joey danced on bare feet over the warm boards, his black eyes sparking with excitement. Then he pushed through the screened door into the cool rooms of the grocery. He was back in a minute with icy Cokes and Almond Joys, Mars Bars, and Baby Ruths he passed out like awards.

Worn out, glowing with success, they sat, legs dangling. Across the alley Mrs. Fenton hung laundry, huge coarse sheets, white and wet and cool as clouds. Clothespins poked from her wide, friendly mouth. Her half-blind collie, Mr. Toot, trotted after her, snapping at the wind-blown sheets as if they were jack-rabbits. Zath looked down at her scuffed Mary Janes. Blood crusted a skinned knee.

She would give up shoplifting, she thought, if she had a boyfriend like Joey, whose family owned a store. He would give her candy and bottles of perfume and the assorted plastic and rubber riches that lay on the deep, deep shelves. In return she would offer him smiles and a clear look at her skirt up across her knees and foot turned just so and a kiss when he hugged her in the dark of the upper balcony at the Crescent. A regular fairy-tale life, she dreamed, watching Mr. Toot lunge at a great billowing sail of sheet and miss.

"What are you gonna do with that?" Joey asked.

"This thing?" She held aloft a few feet of hose. The rest had been pulled away in a tug-of-war. "Keep it as a souvenir. I have a box for stuff like this. Matchbooks and circus tickets. This'll always remind me we won the Battle of Vignola's Lot."

"And the brass thing?"

"The mouthpiece? It's pretty special."

She twisted the mouthpiece from the sewing spool and laid it in his hand. He searched his pockets until he came up with a length of string, threaded it through the brass aperture, tied the ends together, and looped it over her head. It lay against her chest like a *Croix de Guerre*.

"I'm going to learn to play. I mean really play. Not the hose but a real horn."

"You play fine now."

"You're joking."

"Who's joking? You were terrific. A regular Harry James."

"Yeah?"

"Yeah."

"You'll see, I'll get better. I'll take lessons and practice for hours and hours. 'Ebb Tide.' 'I'm Confessin'.' 'Heartbreak Hotel.' I'll play them all."

How long must she practice before she was good enough to

take on Mozart and those other classical guys? Years and years, probably. But she dreamed of that virtuoso hose stunt and longed to be as good as Dennis Brain. Here was someone you had to respect. She wanted to meet him. Maybe his parents owned a store! She had no way of knowing that driving his sports car to a concert, foot to the floor, the top-down roadster held together like his horn with Scotch tape and spit, Dennis Brain had sped into a fog bank and not come out the other side. Would it have made a difference? Possibly. She might have mourned a little and gotten on with life. Then again, maybe she'd have given up horn-playing, slipped behind the wheel of her papa's Hudson Hornet, and taken up drag racing on country roads. It was what you knew and when, it seemed, that determined things. Or maybe you were born knowing.

"Here's to it," said Joey.

They clinked their Coke bottles and drank deeply. When she'd finished, Zath held her bottle to the light. A chalky residue swam at the bottom.

"I dropped an aspirin in yours," Joey said.

"Huh?"

"Soon as it hits, you'll be drunk as anything. You won't know what happened. You'll be laughing and rolling around and having a fit. You'll think I'm hot stuff."

"I already think you're hot stuff."

Mrs. Fenton finished hanging her laundry. The big sheets billowed and cracked in the wind. Mr. Toot made a final half-hearted pass at a shadowy rabbit, then nosed up the back steps and pawed the screen.

DESERT MUSIC

That's Gladys Rose on the carpet, legs above her head, the pink balls of her heels pressing wallpaper of purest eggshell blue. From his vantage in the dinette, Barney sees that despite the puffiness and the blue squiggles of her veins, Gladys Rose still has pretty good legs.

Gladys Rose wants to know what Barney plans to do with his retirement. This afternoon, down at Ferrucci Casting they gave him a Hallmark card, a gold watch and a pat on the back. The card bore twenty-seven signatures. The watch is gold-filled with Japanese works and has a digital readout he can't see without his glasses. "Will it be marathoning?" Gladys Rose asks. "Cordon Bleu cooking? Raising chinchillas so we can be rich as your mother? Or serious drinking? You could become a lush like your brother-in-law Viking Karl."

"Leave Viking Karl out of this, Gladys Rose. I'm touchy where Viking Karl is concerned."

"Viking Karl and your mother. You're a little touchy about her, too. And mention of your sister Wanda doesn't exactly send you to the outer edges of Nirvana. You've a most peculiar family, my darling. Fidelity in lockstep. You just can't shake loose."

"Maybe shaking loose isn't what family life is all about, Gladys Rose. Shaking loose is for running backs looking for long yardage; for seven-foot centers going up for slam-dunks. What I'm saying, Gladys Rose, is that maybe shaking loose is a muscular thing, not to be confused with matters of the heart, the soul."

Barney is drinking Mickey's Big Mouth Beer. The bottle, squat, green, open-mouthed, clutched tightly in his fist, gives the appearance of a bullfrog emerging from primordial ooze.

Barney and Gladys Rose have been together thirty-four years. The house is almost paid off, the Plymouth their own. They have two children: Wally and Ruth.

A thickset bruiser with a palatal defect that makes him hiss his esses, Wally lives in California, and talks of demotions as if they were advancements, firings as if the loss of a job is another stride into a brilliant future. He phones at hours certain to bring Barney and Gladys Rose from deep sleep into wakeful terror. On the bed's edge in the dawn chill they listen as the charges, as if by legal writ, are reversed, then as their only son describes a ruinous life in terms of honesty, uniqueness and bravery. "Maybe we're missing his point," Barney says when the phone is cradled. "He'll hijack an airplane," Gladys Rose speaks into the dimness. "With forged papers and a valise crammed with dynamite. Up the ramp and along the aisle, he'll elbow the flight attendant off-balance, then lunge through the cockpit door. He'll wire a sawed-off shotgun to the pilot's head and demand to be flown to some God-awful fascist state where the generalissimo in charge will pin a medal on Wally's Members Only windbreaker, then declare him Minister of Justice. That's the success I see. Our son: the newest member of the anti-universe."

Ruth will never hijack a plane, nor will she be anyone's Minister of Justice. A slight girl with a nervous cough and mild eyes, she lives on the farthest edge of a Western state with a man who is not her husband. Each year she sends photos of herself and an ever increasing brood of illegitimate children. The man never appears. Maybe he snaps the shutter, though to Gladys Rose the pictures seem not taken at all. They're more like the work of some fey imagination, thin skies and weightless faces washed onto the paper with a scant brush.

"Soul is music," she says from the floor.

Barney sips his beer. "Soul is a spiritual thing," he says. "The essential element."

"Soul is food. Chitterlings, black-eyed peas, fried chicken, watermelon. All the things we were told black people love to eat. Turnip greens and fatback. Truth is, black people like steak and pineapple yogurt like everyone else. They listen to Willie Nelson and play viola for the Boston Symphony. There is no such thing as soul, my darling. It's vanished. A gone commodity, like God's eyes and the I-Ching."

"It's the principle of life and feeling. An entity separate from the body."

"The neon lights of soul have all gone out. One by one. The avenue is deserted. The last dark beauty has gone home."

Barney finishes his beer, then holds the empty bottle to his lip, blowing softly. A sound escapes, deep and throaty, a moan rising from the bottle's neck, thick as eider, bandaging him in breathy music—a sigh of breezes, a blare of southern scorchers, siroccos leveling dunes, combing the sands of endless deserts. Cleansing. Purifying. Soul winds. They're out there, real as anything, though Barney's never heard them, never seen that emptiness. More real, by far, than his cubicle at the foundry, the slack ace of Charley Ferrucci awash in his pink-gummed grin. The Gobi. Atacama. Kalahari. He blows a little longer, his upper lip, as if bee-stung, protruding so that his breath shoots downward into green glass. He plays a melody, a sharp little riff, then again slides into desert music. Lut and Thar. Sonoran. The Kara-Kum and Ar Rab al Khali.

"You know something," Gladys Rose says. Her legs tremble, the beckoning stamens of the flower of which her skirt is the petals.

"I can't be sure," he says, then explains that he won't be running marathons, rustling up gourmet meals or boozing like Viking Karl.

Gladys Rose lowers her legs and sits up, her face suffused with white pulsing stars as the blood flows into her body. "You won't become a *haus frau*. Promise?"

"I've a notion, nothing more."

"No life sentences. No awaiting our executions here on Death Row."

"It's vague. Just a glimmer. A shape taking shape. A kind of fog with form."

"If the fog thickens I'll send out a search party."

"I'm serious, Gladys Rose."

"So am I, my darling. Helicopters, search and rescue teams, St. Bernards with casks of brandy. We'll spare no expense. Till then, save it, Barney. Gladys Rose needs to get on with her life."

Wearing headphones and ball caps, cassette decks slung at their shoulders, they descend the Great Defile. Stalactites, it's explained, are the icicle-shaped deposits of lime suspended from the cavern's roof. Stalagmites, the opposite. They see the Rainbow Bridge, the Bottomless Gorge, the Cathedral of the Bats. It takes a long time. The air, humid, cool, filled with a powerfully sweet fragrance they take to be guano, is still, the cave utterly silent. Only the gibbering voice in the headphones that keeps them from hollering out for the sheer relief of hearing something in this vast, underground waste. Barney pushes his mother's wheelchair;

then Viking Karl takes over.

On the surface, they blink in the brightness, then flip down the plastic sunglasses on the bills of their baseball caps.

The caps are silver and turquoise, matching the paint on the motor home Barney bought the day they sold the house and the Plymouth. Gladys Rose had cried, threatened divorce, suicide, to commit Barney to an asylum. But once he coaxed her inside and showed her the sparkle of plastic and Formica, the ingeniousness of household devices that folded away, sank out of sight, collapsed, fit one into another like painted Russian dolls, self-cleaning gadgetry that appeared when summoned, then vanished on command, she became a convert, won not so much by visions of wheels, the open road and freedom as by the drug of function.

Viking Karl and Wanda have come along for the ride. They have a history of coming along for rides: short rides, long rides, most particularly free rides. As they mount the trail from the cave's mouth to the rock shop, Wanda is a woman in possession of liquid motion, wet eyes, glossed lips with lives of their own. Viking Karl is tight and dry, pony feet in narrow little cowboy boots, mustache skimmed to a froth in a touching tribute to manhood.

Posed back at the motor home, they have their photo snapped, the Indian woman from the rock shop obliging with Barney's mother's Polaroid, fluttering a brown hand to direct them forward, then back, to close ranks, link arms, smile. They engage in similar maneuvers at each stop. It's Barney's mother's idea that Polaroid will supersede all need to remember.

Barney drives with the dreamy inattention they have come to expect: vague crossings of double lines, curves meandered through with casual grace. Sometimes he gets lost, turning from numbered highways onto dirt tracks that lead into wastes of scrub and cactus. He makes no effort to explain these whimsical detours. Convinced to go back, he searches out wide spots in the road in which to turn around. Once, caught at the end of a narrow canyon, the wheels spinning in sand tracked by snakes and asterisks left by lizards' feet, he backs mile after mile, head cocked out the side window, and finally arrives on a paved road none of them has ever seen before.

His mother rides beside him, her wheelchair jockeyed against his seat, a map spread on her lap; in her fingers the photos marking their progress: west, south, then further south.

Bursts of talk pepper the silences. Barney's mother's good ear is skewed to catch conversations on the merciless heat or the beauty of a landscape she views as a lunar horror. Barney has a duty, he feels, to hold the others' attention, plan their campsites and diversions, then propel them through these distances from one shapeless event to another.

"There's a reptile farm not far ahead."

"We saw one already." Barney's mother is a woman of exteriors: glossy still, fussed over, groomed, a husk on which the baseball cap rides like Indian jewelry. Though her fingers are stiffened with arthritis, she has no trouble picking the right snapshot from among the others. "Here. Day before yesterday. Enchanted Mesa Snake Farm. Sidewinders. Copperheads. Diamondbacks. We saw them all."

"We'll skip it if you want. Few miles farther, though, there's a ghost town. You'll like that. Wild West shootouts. Boot Hill. The assayer's office displaying nuggets, coins, gold dust."

Mention of gold draws Viking Karl from the dim middle of the motor home the way a pump draws water. His itch for money is nearly as keen as his lust for booze. Though his knowledge of high finance is strictly secondhand, he never misses a chance to push his views. Settling beside Barney's mother he advises she invest her savings in gold. "Kruggerands, Bullion. Ingots. Listen to me. You can't go wrong."

Barney's mother's laughter is sharp but not quite sensible. "Now tell me, Viking Karl, do you just like to hear yourself talk or are you a representative of the Union of South Africa? Or, maybe, a spokesman for the London Bullion Market?" A smile cracks the barroom gloom Viking Karl wears like a tent. His eyes roll skyward in frustration as if he's humoring a geriatric loony.

An evenness, directness, simplicity, an astonishing logic pervades, an ongoing uncluttered emptiness Barney suspected would be here all along. The desert, planes of gray advancing toward cinnamon buttes, is not a disappointment. When his father was killed by a power-driven ripsaw at the Elvira Box Works, Barney's mother waited a respectful six months, then married a man she had once worked for, a childless widower with a split-level on Park Lane, investments, a pair of heart attacks behind him and another on the way. It came while he was at the wheel of his two-toned Chrysler, the sudden jolt that sent his chins bobbing onto his chest and the car careening off the road. He was pinned to the bottom of a farm pond, the cream and aqua carcass of his car bloated as a drowned cow, wheels uppermost in mossy water.

"Have you become an investment analyst while my back was turned, Viking Karl?" Barney's mother's eyes narrow. "The last time we spoke, if I'm not mistaken, you'd lost a job selling glass bread knives. Before that, you failed with that gadget that made automobiles run on chicken droppings. Earlier, if memory serves, you were turned down—God knows why—by the CIA. Now it seems you would advise me on the purchase of gold. You're a real barroom entrepreneur, Viking Karl. A regular Bill Gates of bourbon and branch water."

Viking Karl looks grave and deeply concerned, frown lines bracketing his tight little mouth, an ironic shadow drifting across his eyes—the kind of look you expect from a car salesman cataloguing a customer's doubts about a junker he's going to wind up buying in the end.

Leaving the others in the shade of the awning, Barney climbs a trail cut into the face of a cliff. Beneath the honey crust are levels of blue and lavender, pale shades of green creating a color he's never seen before. The trail doubles back and he's breathless when he reaches the top where dwellings stand, apartments of sun-dried brick honeycombed under a rock overhang smoothed by water and wind. Doors are cut here and there; windows open into dim rooms; tiered walls rise toward soaring stone. No one has lived here for a long time—five hundred, maybe a thousand years. Still you might, with a bedroll, sticks for fire and a canteen of water, survive.

He sits with his back to a wall, the sun hot on his face. A door stands opened to his left, a shadow in baked mud.

Below, beside the motor home, they talk, smoke extra-long filter-tips, move sluggishly in the heat. Gladys Rose, her feet up, watches Viking Karl pour another tall bourbon while Wanda dreams of hoofing it down to the Union 76 to dance a little soft-shoe for the Minutemen on duty.

Rigid in her steel chair, its spoked wheels a mockery to motion, Barney's mother waits, biding her time, knowing that the advantage, ultimately, for whatever it's worth, lies with her.

Between the walls on either side of Barney a street opens, smooth as though laid out yesterday, straight and true as plane geometry: points, lines, angles, figures in space. Over the lip of the cliff the desert sinks away, vanishing where tall white cumulus build and rebuild themselves against the horizon.

Two days later they cross the border and camp in a patch of dust behind a tin-roofed cantina. Music comes from inside; yowling mariachi issues from an antique jukebox. An electric cord snakes from the cantina, crossing the dust to the motor home where a rotisserie turns a pork loin over smoldering charcoal. The TV beams local news from Phoenix: kids on cocaine; a commodities dealer holding a tennis pro hostage, barricaded in a luxury Scottsdale condo.

When the news ends Gladys Rose switches off the set and gazes into the empty screen. "One Easter we bought him a bunny," she says. "He was five years old. A cute little blond kid in a junior railroad engineer's outfit."

Viking Karl builds another tequila sunrise while Wanda brushes her nails with savage pink lacquer. They know what's coming. Bent above the barbecue Barney spreads sauce on the pork loin, hearing fat sizzle onto the coals and the music from the cantina sweep across the desert. His mother clutches her snapshots and watches Gladys Rose with a vacuity that's both complex and simple as saintliness.

"He had a cap I'd made from pillow ticking and a red neckerchief," Gladys Rose says, turning from the TV to face Viking Karl and Wanda, then Barney, and at last his mother, tilting toward her so their faces almost touch in the twilight. "He was holding the bunny in his arms and we asked what he'd like to name it. 'Fluffy, maybe? Or Snowy? Or Floppy?' He said he wasn't sure. He needed time to think. A five-year-old and he needed time to think what to call a bunny. In his room he put together pieces of the Leggo set we gave him that Christmas. The bunny was in his box, wriggling its nose at the world, crunching carrots. Wally was making things for the bunny, he said. He made the bunny a fort. He made the bunny a tank. He made the bunny a Sidewinder missile, a rocket launcher and a B-52. When he finished the bunny's arsenal, Wally said he'd decided on a name. 'War Bunny,' he told us. 'The rabbit's name is War Bunny!' One night soon we'll switch on the TV and see he's hijacked an airplane."

She stops and the mariachi takes over. Barney watches as she lifts her hands to her face, pressing the sagged flesh. When she speaks again she so perfectly imitates the drawling newscaster that they turn to see the set's off and it's really Gladys Rose saying: "Word has just reached our studio that an unemployed drifter, identified by authorities as Wallace Flowers, has forced his way into the cockpit of American Airlines flight 452 bound for Istanbul, wired a sawed-off shotgun to the pilot's head, and demanded the plane be flown to an as yet undisclosed destination."

"Who are they?"

"Who are who, Mother?"

It's late, the cantina silent, its lights out. The desert has slipped into an envelope of darkness, wind leaking softly at its edges.

"These people. These pictures. Why am I holding them?"

"You wanted them, don't you remember? They're a record of our journey."

"I know that, but do I know them?"

Barney and his mother sit side by side under the awning. The others are in bed. A lantern burns on the table, embers smolder in the barbecue. Barney opens his mother's fingers and takes the photos. "Here are Viking Karl and Wanda." He holds a picture to the light. "That's you and, on the other side, Gladys Rose and me. This was at Alkali Wells. That's a corner of the coffee shop just beyond the motor home. I'm sure it's Alkali Wells."

Barney's mother looks at the picture without seeing it. Her eyes are open but where once they held a cold light they are now muddied and unfocused. "It doesn't matter in the least."

"What?"

"Any of it. It's not important. What difference where we've been? Why explain? Sometimes, Barney, you go too far. You're too accommodating. May I tell you? You're like a headwaiter, figuring what people want, then giving it. They want to talk, you listen. They need coddling, you coddle. Your father wasn't like that. He was a taker, bullying people until he got what he wanted. There were women besides me: floozies upstairs at the Arvenel Hotel, colored girls across the tracks. Bookies threatening to break his thumbs. Tavernkeepers dunning him for year-old tabs. All loving him, of course, that was the thing. Everyone was crazy about Jimmy Flowers."

"He was a pretty rotten father, really."

"That didn't stop you from loving him."

"Maybe."

"People like him always find love. How about you? You must have some reason for pleasing people. You must get something back, some satisfaction. You gave Ferrucci Casting what it wanted; and Gladys Rose and Wanda and that sleazy rat Viking Karl, and me. You want to know what I think? I don't suppose so but I'll tell you anyway: it's because you haven't a clue in the world what you want for yourself. There's an empty place in you, Barney. What the star people call a black hole. I thought you should know."

But this trip is for Barney. Every inch of it. Beyond the awning the night sky streams down, black as buckets of hot tar. Stars, more than he's ever seen, though he doesn't know their names, can't name a single constellation. After all those years in factory towns, he had to come and see this. Maybe the emptiness is only echoing something in himself. He doesn't know. What he does know is that it feels right, as if he's spent a lifetime preparing for this. He stretches, breathing in sage-scented air, then leans forward and snuffs the lantern. "It's late, Mother."

As he wheels her to the top of the ramp she lifts a hand to stop him.

"Who was it she was talking about?"

"Who, Mother?"

"Gladys Rose. Was it Gladys Rose?"

"It was Gladys Rose."

"And the boy with the bunny?"

"Wally, Mother. Your grandson, Wally Flowers."

"Why don't I see him? If he's my grandson, why isn't he here?"

"He's away on business, Mother. California. He has a great many responsibilities."

"He travels, is that it?"

"A bit, yes."

"Flies American to Turkey and the Middle East."

"Exactly."

"Is he CIA, Barney? Is he a secret agent the way Viking Karl wanted to be?"

"We don't know, Mother. He can't say."

"It's hush-hush?"

"Hush-hush."

"She misses him. That's why she carried on the way she did."

"We all miss him."

"Will you tell him I want to see him? Write and ask him to come. We'll have Christmas. The whole family. Doesn't matter when. We'll have presents, a tree, turkey with all the trimmings."

Barney pushes the wheelchair up the ramp, helps his mother into bed. When he bends to kiss her goodnight she clutches his hand.

"Does anyone know where we are?"

"Mexico, Mother. We crossed the border a couple of days ago."

"Mexico? You never were one to stay home and tend to business."

"I stayed home all my life, Mother."

"Then why are you here?"

Viking Karl has finally grown into his boots. "Now listen, everyone," he says, taking charge, "here's what you've got to do."

Barney put water on for coffee, punched holes in a can of Donald Duck orange juice, checked to see that the electric cord was plugged in at the back of the cantina. The music hadn't started yet, but it wouldn't be long. Then he looked in on his mother and found her dead. It happened, probably, moments after he kissed her goodnight.

"Do you know what this means?" Viking Karl puts on his hat, huge and ridiculous, though its brim is sloped at a defiant angle. "Do you have the slightest idea?"

Catching sight of her mother slumped into a corner of her bunk, Wanda dissolves, useless to anyone. Face down in the leatherette booth, she bawls uncontrollably.

"She passed away." Gladys Rose looks up from the booth where she comforts Wanda. "Gone. Just as she promised."

"It's not that simple." Viking Karl cocks a hand on his hip. "Do you realize where we are? Look around, Mrs. Sure-of-yourself. This is Mexico. M-E-X-I-C-O. You don't 'pass away' in Mexico. You don't just 'go'. Not if you're some fool gringo down here for the cheap pesos and fast times. It's what they have jails for—fool gringos. This is a land of jails; the place where jails were invented. Perfected down to the last detail. They've got special varieties of vermin just to withstand the harsh conditions. It takes something special to survive the mud floors and filth, the bad water and beans."

"You're clearly an expert."

"I get around. I hear things. It doesn't take much imagination."

"But isn't it a little late?" Glady's Rose, patting the sobbing

—23—

Wanda, looks up at Viking Karl. "If you ask me, the person in question is beyond jail."

Barney stands at the stove trying to make coffee, turning on and off the flame, the flickering blue pompon fading and dying, then blossoming again. Stunned, he supposes. Deep in shock. On the other hand, things seem quite clear—Viking Karl and Gladys Rose's conversation, for instance, which he hears with an almost prescient lucidity, knowing the words, the forms they'll take even before they've spoken. His mother has died so many times in his imagination that the actual event is charged with a strong dose of deja vu. Wanda's noisy bawling. The airlessness. The sensation that his body, stiff as a department store mannequin, is a stranger outside his control. Even the Sonoran outback and the sudden absurd blast of jukebox mariachi fail to dispel the feeling that he's lived through this before.

"I'm talking about us," Viking Karl declares. "You and me and Barney and Wanda. We're in possession of the deceased. It isn't safe to be in possession of the deceased in a land of jails and brown barbarians. They have ways of dealing with people. And if we don't end up in jail or being fed to the ants, we're sure to wind up in a bureaucratic jungle that'll keep us here forever."

"For someone who's been here an entire day-and-a-half," Gladys Rose says, "you have some pretty strong opinions."

"I know what I know."

"Nothing new."

"And I know we need documentation, a doctor, death certificate, export papers allowing us to take the body back to the States."

"You mean real problems."

"You admit it!"

"Difficulties, at any rate."

"It's impossible to file a last will and testament in a U.S. court if you can't present a death certificate, if that's what you mean by

—24—

difficulties. And a death certificate can't be had if the person in question, the deceased, isn't present for competent authorities to examine, but is, instead, dragged from pillar to post by a pack of half-mad Mexican lawyers and petty officials who only want to keep us from taking Mother Flowers back to her homeland for decent burial."

"Touching."

"Exactly, Gladys Rose."

"Especially the bit about the last will and testament."

"It's important to us all."

"And your point is, I take it, that we have to spirit—is that the word?—spirit Mother Flowers back to her homeland without the Mexicans knowing?"

The road north, Mexico's Route 2, is pure disaster. Claro. Carborca. Costa Rica. Quitovac. The towns lined by chuckholes and ruts and a spring thaw of chunked-up asphalt adrift in rivers of dust. Viking Karl chooses the way and does the driving, his cowboy boots barely reaching the pedals as he jerks the motor home into lurching, side-slipping submission.

Just before dawn they reach Sonoyata: shopfronts shadowed by cinder block arcades, a dog nosing truck tires, aging Chevrolets. Gladys Rose pronounces it a likely place. "Just over there!" She gestures toward a shaded wall. *Cervezas y Comidas.* "Hat tugged low, bandoleers—is that the word?—bandoleers crossed on his chest, a gun the size of Viking Karl's left leg."

"No one's there, Gladys Rose."

"Mean lookin' hombre. Lean and mean. Twirling a toothpick under his blond mustache. Eyeing us. A hard blue stare. I'd know those eyes anywhere. Hard and blue. I see those eyes every minute of my life."

"It's a shadow, Gladys Rose. Sun-up playing with shadows."

"A shadow, definitely. A shadow among shadows."

The shadow turns out to be a policeman who accompanies them the hundred yards to the border, walking ceremoniously beside the motor home, one hand on the butt of his gun, the other resting on the window ledge beside Viking Karl's shoulder as if leading some huge beast to an appointment at the *abattoir*.

At the frontier they file into a pink splash of morning. Viking Karl leads Wanda by the arm. Barney and Gladys Rose come next, wary as felons ready to jerk their coats over their heads at the first sign of a camera. Yet, as if Barney's mother were still giving orders, they line up as though waiting for the click of the Polaroid. Just above their heads the furled awning bulges with contraband.

This crazy stuff is part of Viking Karl's plan. A bend in his cloak-and-dagger imagination: riding the Mexican backcountry with Barney's mother's corpse rolled in the awning. When they reach Phoenix, Viking Karl envisions an unveiling ceremony before a gathering of authorities as Mother Flowers is unleashed and exposed. First they must deal with this lineup of Mexican cops, scratching and yawning, blowing fat clouds of smoke from brown cigarettes, eyeing them like some casual firing squad ready for a morning's work.

"We were never more than four!" Viking Karl stretches his neck, standing on tiptoe, hollering this into the face of a cop with gold braid and mirrored glasses. The two men float toe to toe, a pair of boozy salts plying a familiar tequila sea: "You can count: *uno*, *dos*, *tres* . . ."

"We have no interest in counting."

". . . *cuatro*".

"We have no interest in you." The man speaking English wears a soiled brown suit and bush hat. He stands beside the cop with gold braid, coolly eyeing Viking Karl.

Viking Karl dances toward him, then backpedals a step.

"Why have you stopped here?" the brown suit demands.

"You want to leave Mexico, go. We have no interest. Please keep moving."

Across the road, beyond the thicket of tin-roofed shacks, junked cars and children playing in narrow spaces between buildings, back where the desert rides east through a vastness so compelling Barney can't tear himself from it, the sun clears the horizon. Shading his eyes, he glimpses Viking Karl bouncing nervously on tiptoe, dashing forward, bobbing and weaving like a hotshot bantamweight.

"We won't be pushed around," he shrills. "We're American citizens. We know our rights. You're not bullying."

"But we have no interest."

"There's nothing to hide. Understand? You want to search, search. We're not afraid. Look all you want. We've nothing to hide."

"Señor, please you do not."

"Macho Mexicans think you're such hot cops"

The flash of a soiled brown sleeve. The bush hat retreats to the back of the man's head, then tugged forward and adjusted, the brim arranged just so, the gesture no more threatening than any habitual reaction to fraying nerves. As the brim comes to rest at a precise angle across the dark brow, the phalanx of policemen begins to move. They edge heavily forward, reluctant to begin body searches and the tedious work of ransacking cupboards and closets, rooting through the stained garments of perfect strangers.

"Anyway, the awning idea turned out okay. Perfect, really. No one had a clue."

"There were clues. A whiff of death, if nothing more. If one of them had had an ounce of curiosity, it would have taken some fast thinking to shake them off."

"Viking Karl would have come up with something."

"Yeah, I had a few things left up my sleeve."

Hat cocked over a wise-guy eye, Viking Karl pushes the motor home through the curves, presses it down the straight-aways, highballing cross country, homeward bound. On the outskirts of Ajo, Arizona he brakes for a truck stop.

It's a long walk up the roadside through diesel fumes and afternoon heat. Indians, war parties of them, patrol back and forth in muddy pickups. Tourists in Winnebagos. Trailing the others, Barney watches the little dust storms kicked up by Viking Karl's boots.

Inside, it's noisy with truckers' chaff and country music. Deep in a booth, Wanda and Viking Karl and Gladys Rose eat double chili burgers and platters of home fries, while Barney sips weak tea, wondering what he's doing here. He feels no need of food but is pleased to see the others eating. They deserve this consolation of spiced meat and fried potatoes. Especially the women: Wanda for losing her mother, Gladys Rose for losing her son. Alas, Wally was not wandering the backstreets of Mexico.

"They have hair dye," she said, studying each cop as he mounted the ramp and filed into the motor home. "Hair dye and contact lenses that change the color of their eyes. Glue-on mustaches and suntan oil that tints their skin. Who says he's not right here? Who says that's not him digging through Wanda's high style clothes?"

She doesn't believe it.

Neither does Barney.

Any of it.

Sitting back, he listens to the sounds of eating, the drift of voices and plangent songs of loss, a shadow of desert wind leaning against the walls, sighing at every window.

At the far end of the room a pock-faced young Indian in headband and greasy chef's smock thoughtfully pushes a broom across the floor, a certain courageous inefficiency in the way he jabs it under tables, around counter stools, between people's feet without actually disturbing the dirt—as if directing some small, slow-footed animal in a harmless dance. Twirling, he glides downstream with his broom, to the tune of "I'm A Thorn And You're My Country Rose."

After eating, Barney follows the others outside. The wind has risen. A taste of dust and distance fills the air. On the porch the Indian swipes at fast-food trash drifting around the door. Has he seen the honey-colored mesa? Barney wonders. Did his ancestors lay out the streets, chink the bricks with mud and straw? Watch the clouds build on the horizon? Is he even the right kind of Indian? Probably not. Still, he might have tales of honor, sacrifice and survival. On the other hand, they'd probably dribbled away in government beer and tired genes.

But he wants to know. Turns back to ask as Viking Karl hurries toward inquests and probate courts, Wanda and Gladys Rose trailing in his dust. On the porch the Indian watches, his broom suddenly quiet, the dance of the invisible animal halted on point.

THE HORSES SPEAK FRENCH

On the afternoon in Linares when Manolete bled out his life on Islero's horns, it was Luis Varga, El Pantero, who took over the great matador's *caudrilla*, Manolete's handpicked band of picadors and banderilleros. Among their august company, El Pantero suffered bleak dreams of the tragic artist of the *muleta*, the wiry, bad-tempered bull that cut him down.

"It was a Miura bull that killed Manolete," says Doña Carmine. "Bred by Don Eduardo. A terrible man who chose only heifers like him—keelers! He only wanted breed bulls would keel the *toreros*!"

Across the terrace the Indian Ocean spreads like a cloth thrown over the edge of Africa. A dhow scissors across, its sail a pale cursor on the great sea. Sunset. Africa, a dark and empty bowl, lies behind. Benson, Doña Carmine's houseman, pours sherry, a gift sent from Jerez by Carmine's sister. Two small glasses. One for Doña Carmine, one for me.

On a table beside her wheelchair stands a photo taken forty years ago—a svelte young woman in a chic Dior suit. She was what we call "a beauty," sleek, aristocratic, rich. "One day on our ranch where we raised bulls, my godson Diego came to me. He was the son of Consuela, our cook. He said, 'Madrina, are you a man or a woman?'

"'But, of course, Diego, I am a woman. Like your mother and your Auntie Maria and sister Pilar.'

"'But, Madrina, you don't work and you drink wine. I think you are a man.'"

Carmine glances again at the photo. "I was very beautiful," she says with complete confidence. "Not like now." Her beatific smile never leaves her. No one knows what is wrong, but her nerves have come unraveled and her body doesn't obey simple commands. Her hands sometimes flap at improbable angles, then drop heavily into her lap. "Manolete was a great man," she says quietly. "A tragic man. Though he was a friend of my father, I saw him only once when I was ten."

For a dozen dusty summers Manolete's *caudrilla* followed him across the Spanish countryside. After his death they accompanied El Pantero, a grinning Gypsy in a cheap suit who faced bulls with capricious inattention, thinking if he failed to notice them, they wouldn't know he was there.

It was 1959, Hemingway's year to parade across Spain with Antonio Ordóñez and Luis Miguel Dominguin, the matadors of the moment. Ordóñez was "Don Ernesto's" prince, the eminent author following him as if trying to recapture the time of his *duende*, the great years of *The Sun Also Rises* and *Death in the Afternoon*. In Pamplona for the *feria* of San Fermin, he bragged and belted champagne in the smoke and noise of the Cafe Irun. I finally found a table across the room, but in the clamor failed to distinguish a word of Papa's slurred monologue. Next day at the Plaza de Toros, I mounted a cheap seat high in the sun, while Hemingway had the prime place, surrounded by admirers in a shady box on the *barrea*. Close beside him a woman spoke in his ear: Doña Carmine. The photo appeared in *Paris Match* the following week. Now it rests in a sterling frame on the table beside her chair.

"What did you say to him," I ask as the tropical dusk falls like a Somali shawl thrown over us. "I spoke of Antonio Ordóñez." Carmine looks at the picture and laughs. "You see, Ordóñez is about to dedicate the bull to Hemingway. 'Don Ernesto,' I told him, 'you know it's Antonio without seeing his face—he has such ugly legs.' Hemingway didn't like. You see how sour he looks."

With bravery and skill, Ordóñez and Dominguin confronted huge Benítez Cubero bulls that day, fierce and unforgiving as locomotives. With the famous author looking on, the crowd grew delirious, stamping, cheering, drowning the afternoon in ¡Oles!

Though his *caudrilla* was splendid, the banderilleros perfection, the picadors' work light and dangerous, El Pantero, third matador of the cartel, disappointed. Agile enough to dodge swift bulls but preoccupied. A sleepwalker. With Hemingway on the *barrea* and Dominguin and Ordóñez triumphant, it was unforgivable, perilous. When his second bull caught him musing, nudging him with the flat of a horn, you could hear the crack of Gypsy ribs. Manolete's *caudrilla* swept in with their capes to save the dreamy panther a deadly goring.

"They were all flamencos—Manolete's old *caudrilla*," Doña Carmine says. "Manolete himself hoped to dance, not fight bulls. If things had worked out, he might have lived a few more than his thirty years."

El Pantero was another flamenco. In the panting African night I can almost hear his Gypsy strumming. Toledo: a room down the hall. The buzz of the panther's guitar hauntingly familiar. In the stuffy hotel the banderilleros snapped their fingers, banged their heels; the picadors tore the air with Gypsy cries; the perfumed barber, posed in the open doorway, struck an extravagant tambourine. Toledo's streets dozed under a broiling sun. Along dim corridors the walls of the old hotel sighed with expectations of siesta. I swam all morning in the Rio Tajo, surfed the falls boiling over the ancient weir to the beach under the Moorish bridge. In a thatched lean-to a somber old woman cooked over an open fire. I ate *arroz con pollo*, drank spicy sangria poured from a cracked jug. After a beaker of strong coffee, I hiked steep streets to my hotel. To hell with Hemingway. In town for the *corrida*, talking endlessly of his achievements to the wearying Ordóñez, the eminent author had nothing on me.

The barber woke me, his lush cologne smoking through the open door to wrap me up like a bandit. Crooking a finger, he beckoned me from the hot stupor of a half-finished siesta. "Come quick! These horses in the room of El Pantero—they spic only the French." Down the hall came Gypsy yelps and a muscular ring of flamenco guitar. I followed the barber into the dim suite where El Pantero, stripped to the waist, was mounted on a massive bed, his thighs forced into the skin-tight pants of his *Trajes de Luces*, iridescent as the carapaces of rhinoceros beetles. Pink stockings sheathed slim calves, a braided cue clung above a neck dark as a cigar. While banderilleros clapped rhythm and a lone picador bayed an imaginary moon, the guitar sang in El Pantero's hands, menacing and Gypsy quick.

"*Norteamericano!*" he shouted, slamming the instrument into silence. "You must spic these horses—they spic only the French."

Peering into shadow, I saw a vast Spanish room thick with tragedy and ponderous furniture and the men of Manolete's *caudrilla*. No horses, no Rosinante, African zebra or Sicilian donkey, not even the sacrificial nag of a corpulent picador.

Then the women emerged from El Greco gloom. The horses.

Big blondes in chopped skirts and skimpy tops. Anita Eckberg and one of those nameless ravishing beauties from Roger Vadim's stable of ex-wives.

"These horses," the panther said, grinning a Gypsy grin, "are, you know, very *décolletage.*"

Décolletage—like my morning on the river, an ivory plunge into cooling water. The women clung, murmuring in luscious French, a pair of stunning concupiscent saints in the chapel of El Pantero and the *caudrilla* of Manolete.

"These horses spic not the Spanish," the panther said, bouncing from the bed to land flat-footed beside the lovely Miss Eckberg. His muscles tensed, rippling beneath a skin mapped with scars. "Tell these *putas*," he said, breathing into Eckberg's ear, "we will go with them after the *corrida.*"

I tried to explain that they were not horses, not *putas*, but movie stars, actresses famous throughout the world. *La Dolce Vita*, I asked the *torero*, had he not seen Miss Eckberg in the cinema? *La Dolce Vita?*

"I have bulls to kill," said El Pantero, laying a hand on Miss Eckberg's thigh, grinning into the cool abyss of her *décolletage.* "I have not time for the *ciné.* Just tell this *puta* to stick around. I'll go with her after the bulls."

I suggested the matador take time to familiarize himself with Eckberg's performances.

"Good. Fine. Just tell the *puta* to be here."

Before I could trot out my French for a translation of the *torero*'s proposition, the grand impresario Don Ignacio Quintana pushed in, mopping sweat from his hairless dome, snapping orders for the panther to dress quickly for the *corrida.* Then he halted before Eckberg, eyeing the *décolletage.* "Telephone!" Don Ignacio boomed, thrusting his elbow deep within the actress's depending bosoms, talking into his hand. "Telephone! I'm spicking on the telephone!"

Sunlight glanced from his spectacles—the left lens only. A spark catching fire. He wore a cap with a leather bill. A dark and plunging mustache. Behind him, on thick double doors planked in oak, was painted the number 3. Beyond the doors the bull waited in darkness—a great gray *Concha y Sierra* bull from the swamps of Las Marismas on the banks of the Guadalquivir. He was Hormigón, "Concrete," the ultimate bull. The sixth. El Pantero's bull. Light blazed, then vanished from wire-rimmed spectacles. The man in the cap released the door.

Toledo's bullring is small and intimate; its seats mount steeply in a score of rows. Even in a cheap seat near the top I caught the hot glint of the bull's eyes, heard the scuffle of the *toreros'* slippers on the raked sand.

When Hormigón rushed from the *torrell* into the last crescent of sunlight slanting onto the ring, he seemed so incredibly threatening I found myself looking for an escape.

With a sweep of his cape El Pantero drew Hormigón from sunlight into shadow. The bull moved quickly, head lowered, the great lethal curve of his horns trailing the cape in a tight half-circle before plunging back into the narrowing sickle of sunlight. The panther drew him out and took charge, unfolding a series of slow, majestic passes, the bull pursuing the cloth as if he were sewn to it. The crowd cheered, two or three bands accompanying the bedlam.

Then the picadors swayed in aboard their padded nags and the bull charged at once. The first horse shuddered under the impact. Placing his lance on the hump of the bull's great neck, the picador leaned his weight against the shaft. El Pantero drew Hormigón quickly away. Little damage was done. The luck of the draw gave the panther a dream bull and he didn't want it ruined.

Once more the bull charged the horse. El Pantero and the *caudrilla* of Manolete quickly caped the beast away in a flourish of arabesques.

Then El Pantero dismissed his banderilleros, Pepe Gómez and the great Ramón Vazquez, and darted the bull himself. With grace, skill and bravery, he placed the first two pair. The third pair he broke across his knees so they were little more than a foot long. He stood his ground, the abbreviated sticks poised above his head. The panther shifted his body to the left, but not his feet. As the bull charged, he quickly brought his shoulders to the right. As the animal thundered past, barbed him brilliantly with two banderillas. The crowd exploded. Bands roared.

"Where were the women?" Doña Carmine asked. "The horses who spoke French?"

"Eckberg and the other? With Hemingway, of course."

"On the *barrea* in the shade just as I heard."

"You weren't there, Doña Carmine?"

"They were not bulls from our ranch, thank God. I was in Madrid taking sherry with my mother."

On cue, Benson appears to refill our glasses. The wine is a *Domecq Gonz lez*, clear and dry as a desert wind. We toast El Pantero, touching our glasses in the dimness. Beyond the terrace the dhow vanishes across Lamu Bay and a great orange moon rises above Manda Island's mangrove swamps.

"And so," said Carmine, "began the *faena*."

The audience grew hushed when El Pantero stepped forth with his *muleta*. Slowly he tested the bull, strong and brave as ever. Then began a series of linked passes, the panther controlling the animal as he spun with the cloth.

Solid, collected, cool, the Gypsy worked through the repertory of the *muleta* and improvised a pass or two of his own. The crowd roared in admiration.

The panther, taking courage, ended with a sequence of spinning passes. As the bull hurled past, the panther whirled in the direction opposite the charge, drawing the cloth away from the bull and enveloping his own body. It was beautifully done. A virtuoso performance. The blaring of the bands and the cheering crowd left no doubt that El Pantero was giving the performance of his life.

Again silence fell over the ring. El Pantero, with scrupulous care, squared the bull. The panther was ready to strike, foil poised, the bull motionless, filled with energy and rage for the final plunge. The panther's muscles were taut under the suit of lights, the way they tensed and rippled under the scarred skin when he leaped from the bed. Then they went slack, the eyes softened, found the women, the big blonds in the skimpy clothes, one on either side of Hemingway, who tensed forward, his beard a silver ruff at the throat of his open shirt. The women leaned against him, waiting, swaying in the shadows of late afternoon.

AT THE PUNISHMENT CLIFF FOR WOMEN

Beneath a calendar picture of robed pilgrims worshiping at the Kaaba, Arif tilts back in a rush-bottomed chair. He waits, fingers drumming the knees of gleaming white trousers. The room simmers and behind the desk Mr. Akarsu dozes, now and then waking to slap at flies. Every few minutes another truck grinds past on the dark road outside, its headlights sweeping the barred windows. When Maya and Paul open the door from the street, the legs of Arif's chair strike the tiled floor and Mr. Akarsu raises his head, blinks, then his unshaven chin falls back to his chest. Arif crosses to Maya in his soft shoes, takes her arm and leads her into the street. Paul follows.

"Your day was pleasant?" Arif asks.

"Pleasant?" Maya's face is a pale oval in the dimness. "It was fine."

She and Paul had ridden the bus east along the coast through lemon groves and banana plantations. After swimming from the white beach at Side, they found a *dolmus* to drive them inland where they ate at a cafe on the river's edge. Grilled trout, egg-plant, rice. In deep concentration, as if he were a brewmaster awarding medals, Paul drank several bottles of beer. Steps from where they ate, the river dropped in steep rapids. Its roar struck their ears like applause and spray bathed their tanned faces. Even so, it was hot, and Maya longed to strip off her thin dress and float over the falls and out to sea.

"Do you think I could?" she asked, blue eyes turned to the river.

"Could what?" Paul's voice was distant, clouded with beer.

"It doesn't matter." Her thin, pretty face gave nothing away. "Anyway, you wouldn't care if I did."

"If I knew what it was."

"You wouldn't."

An eagle sailed against the cloudless sky. People in shorts and pastel tops took photographs. Maya licked salt from her lips and contented herself watching Paul drink beer. Empty bottles crowded their table like friends.

Arif draws Maya against him as a truck sweeps past, then leads her along the dark road into a lighted boulevard. Paul hurries a few steps behind. Here, stores and cafes are open and people crowd the sidewalks. A horse-drawn cart rattles over the broken pavement, and music pulses from shops selling cassettes. The soulful wailings and throaty sobs that Maya finds exciting make Paul hold his head in pain.

Arif glances over his shoulder. "Why do you stay in that hotel?"

Paul shrugs. "Why not?" he says.

It's the sort of place they always stay. Cheap and near the bus station. There's a tea shop around the corner and a cafe in the next block where meals cost almost nothing.

"It is not nice," Arif says, chopping his words for emphasis.

Dark and tall with a heavy mustache and hooded eyes, Arif met them on the promenade in the public gardens, at a place where limestone cliffs drop two hundred feet into the placid blue of the bay. Paul had arranged Maya against the railing, moving her this way and that. When he had her where he wanted, he stepped back, focusing his camera. As he made a final adjustment Arif stepped into the frame. He pointed to the jagged fall, telling them this was the punishment cliff for women. "They were tied in bags," he said, "those women who sinned, then thrown over the edge."

Maya remained motionless. "What sins? What had they done?"

Arif's dark eyes narrowed, studying Maya for several seconds. "Who knows?" he said. "It was long ago."

Now they hurry, passing shoppers and idlers and the robed women who gather each evening before the lighted windows of the gold shops. Arif rushes. Maya and Paul run to keep up. They turn east at the seafront and enter an unknown part of town.

The restaurant is on the second floor of a modern highrise. A white-jacketed waiter who calls Arif by name escorts them to a table with a view of a tree-lined street. Sometimes a horse-drawn cab clatters past; taxis come and go from the rank near the fountain across the way. A pair of well-dressed men at a nearby table return Arif's greeting. He hails the waiter and orders wine.

The restaurant is crowded. But Maya notices there is only one other woman in the room, at a table in the back near the kitchen. She resembles the women Maya sees in the streets, only thinner, harder edged, with wild hair dyed an intense black and a voice like a weapon aimed at the plump man with the bald sweating head sitting opposite her. Maya wonders if after the meal the woman will be dragged from the restaurant, trussed like a fowl and sailed from the cliff into the Mediterranean. Maya and Paul are the only foreigners.

They drink quickly and begin a second bottle of wine. The music is soft-porn pop. The food, when it arrives, is ordinary. They might be anywhere. Arif begins to talk, to tell his story. To Maya it's predictable; Paul, getting glassy-eyed on the wine, has difficulty following. First is the misunderstanding wife Arif hasn't lived with for years, but whom he hasn't divorced. Under the influence of her brothers, Shi'ite fundamentalists, she is kept in purdah. "She almost never goes out and when she does she's wrapped like a mummy. How can a man love a woman like that, a woman who won't show her body, who won't be free? The worst is, she's raising my daughter to be like her. There's nothing I can do. She won't see me. The child is a stranger."

Across the room the woman has stopped talking; the bald man pats pink lips with a large napkin. How could Arif let such a thing happen? Maya wants to know. Didn't he see it coming? Can't the brothers be stopped? Why doesn't he kidnap the child and take her away?

He claims he left both wife and daughter behind and went to Canada, where he found work as a draftsman. "In Toronto I was cold but happy. Everyone is relaxed, easygoing. There are many beautiful women. People are free. It is a wonderful place."

"How long were you there?"

"Two years."

"Then you came back for your family?"

"I went to Philadelphia, where I met Barbara." She was thirty-four, never married, a school teacher living with her mother. Arif saw her on the steps of the Academy of Music. Tall and slim, a natural blond. He followed her into a Latimer Street coffee shop and introduced himself. "You must have my child," he told her over hot chocolate. "Your blondness, my darkness will make a beautiful son." They dated for a year, but she didn't become pregnant. "I begged for this perfect son, but she said no, it is not right."

She moved from her mother's and shared his furnished room overlooking the Schuylkill River. Each day he walked to work at a nearby architect's studio while Barbara bused to South Philadelphia to teach math to orphan boys. On weekends they locked themselves into his drab room and made love. "It was fantastic. She was beautiful. Best of all, she was free. What we did together was like a dream." But she wouldn't have his child. He insisted. After six months she returned to her mother.

Maya finishes eating and pours more wine. "You can go back now and marry her."

"When I marry it will not be with Barbara."

"No?"

"Love is love, marriage is business. Barbara teaches school. She cares for her mother. She has no money. She cannot buy me a shop."

"A shop?"

"Or cafe. I must have my own business in America. A wife must provide this. It is my dream."

He talks, his voice a deep message, but Maya no longer listens. She fills her glass and drinks deeply. Arif's whimsy of shopkeeping in Philadelphia seems mad enough, but the notion that some future bride will buy him a corner candy store or quicky burger stand is beyond comprehension. Across the table Paul seems to be asleep, his thin, troubled face glowing with sunburn, though now and then he reaches for his glass. He's slightly drunk, Maya observes, a little over his depth. Beside him, Arif at last falls silent.

"You almost got there," Maya tells him.

His smile flickers. He studies his hands. "Almost got where?"

"You don't know? Wherever it was you thought you wanted to go."

"And that is where?"

"Nowhere, it's nothing, forget it."

Arif reaches across the table and grasps her hand. "As you wish."

Suddenly, from across the room, comes a pained cry. The woman with dyed hair is standing unsteadily, head thrown back, arms aloft in a trembling arc. Her voice fills the room. At first Maya thinks of the singer Um Kalthum, the Mother of Egypt, and believes the woman is singing, for the sound is a kind of lament. But the cry goes on and on, rising and falling as the woman sways in the narrow space beside her table. Paul struggles in his chair, eyes wide, mouth twisted. Arif pretends not to notice and clutches Maya's hand. The lamentation continues, becomes a howl, a groan, a soft, ululating whimper. At last it ends and the woman falls exhausted into her chair while her companion mops his perspiring head. Maya shakes off Arif's grip and crosses to her.

It's a joke, of course. What can she do? The woman waves her away. They know nothing of each other, share no common language. The man stares blankly at Maya, then turns his face to the wall. She stands, empty hands at her sides. Everyone is watching.

Back at the table, Paul has gone. A dish stacked with money is at his place. Arif sips the last of the wine.

Maya extends her hand toward the money but doesn't touch it.

Arif puts down his glass. "Your friend left the money. He asked to pay."

"No. I know him better."

Arif opens his arms and smiles. "The boy's had a long day. He's gone back to that wretched hotel, says we're to go on without him."

"On?"

"A place near the public gardens not so far from the cliff where we met. There'll be music and wine. I know the band leader. We can dance."

FERRY FROM KABATAS

A white ship glides across a pink sea. Hamsun is at the railing, watching students crowded amidships, teenagers with a free day, a noisy, easygoing crowd, joking, singing, playing guitars. A teaboy darts among them, passing steaming glasses from his tray, taking payment in the scraps of crumpled lavender paper they use for money here. The young people buy tea for one another, compete at being first to pay. When the tray is empty the teaboy hurries toward the galley, wiping his hands on a stained apron. Hamsun catches his eye, waves and orders tea for himself. He left Robin sleeping at a table in the lounge, her head cradled in her arms. When she wakes she can track down the teaboy herself.

When he's finished his tea and balanced the empty glass on a lifeboat stanchion, Hamsun packs his pipe and smokes. The sun breaks the mist and the sea turns from pink to pale fire. Some teenagers have wandered away, sixteen-year-olds who have discovered love, holding hands. One couple stands near Hamsun, talking quietly, while another stops at the stern where a flag snaps in the wind. The boy is skin-and-bones, wearing what in this part of the world passes for a Hawaiian shirt. He shouts to friends, makes grotesque faces, attempts a halfhearted handstand on the aft railing, then holds the girl against him, kissing her when he manages to turn her face toward him, running his hand under her shirt. She pushes him away, laughing. She's small, Hamsun notices, with fine bones and dark hair. When, tussling good-naturedly with the boy, she turns and faces Hamsun, he sees how pretty she is—more than pretty. She knows he's watching and smiles, then throws herself on the boy, kissing him wildly on the mouth.

"Excuse me, I wish to be apologizing"

"Beg your pardon?"

"For the most unfortunate behaviors."

He's smaller than Hamsun, smaller and darker, but that's not surprising when you consider how swollen and inflamed Hamsun appears, how like thick Scandinavian bread cooked in too hot an oven. The new man has black wavy hair slicked to his skull and a mustache from an earlier century. Nearing thirty, his name is Ersine, and he's returning home to Diyarbakir.

"I am Kurd," he says, punching his chest. He wears a dark suit with a dress shirt buttoned at the throat, but no tie. "In Diyarbakir are Kurdish peoples. In Diyarbakir are young people not behaving scandalous as you are seeing here."

"I'm not sure I understand."

"Young girls dressing in shorts, singing and dancing in public, making love with boys not their husbands. Very bad are city girls not caring for religion, girls not covering their heads." He makes a gesture with his hands, not the wavy hourglass traditionally used to describe a woman's body but a brusque motion of dismissal. Then he smiles radiantly, orders tea for the two of them and offers Hamsun a cigarette. "Maltepe," he says. "Mostly excellent Turkish tobaccos."

As they drink tea and smoke, Hamsun wonders what Robin

will make of Ersine. The man has strong features, lively black eyes, a mouthful of amazingly white teeth—all high on Robin's list of desirable qualities and about as different from Hamsun as she could find. He feels uneasy. She's someone who can't resist comparisons. He hopes she'll sleep all morning or find a place to sunbathe so that he can avoid an introduction.

What Ersine will make of her is another matter. A strawberry blond half Hamsun's age, she was wearing, when they boarded before dawn, a hot-pink bikini bottom and lime-green tank top. Why she hasn't frozen in the cool sea air Hamsun can't imagine. When they first met in early May she'd stepped out of an icy, squall-dark sea onto the windy beach at Carpathos, then stood among the rocks talking with him without a shiver. Thick skin, though you wouldn't think it to look at her.

A ship bears down on them, a black-hulled freighter. Ersine takes Hamsun's arm and leads him across the deck and forward to the top of the companionway for a better view. "Roossian," he says, pointing. "Very big. Going for Odessa, I am thinking." The ship slides silently past. "You are going far?"

"Yalova," Hamsun answers.

"Ah." Ersine nods gravely. "And from Yalova?" A traveler, Hamsun does not enjoy talk of travel. Over the years he has wearied of too many conversations in which participants try to outscore one another in the game of who's been where. Where he goes from Yalova will not interest him until he is there. Still, he has accepted tea and cigarettes from Ersine. He cannot be rude. He tells the Kurd he will go on by bus to Urgup.

"Ah, Cappadocia. Very interesting is Cappadocia. You travel with your wife?"

The Russian freighter passes. For several minutes the ferry from Kabatas rocks wildly in its wake, then settles to cautious progress, its engines thrumming dully below. From where he stands Hamsun sees past a corner of the pilot house to the forward deck, where women use crates and bales as benches. A poorly lashed boom sways from side to side above their heads. In colorless head scarves and coats reaching to their shoe tops, the women look like cargo themselves, bags of cheap goods, bundles of someone's belongings left behind in a disaster. In a distant corner near the forecastle bulkhead, lying in a patch of sunlight no larger than her body, Robin rests her blond head on her rucksack and dozes. She's slipped up her tank top and bared her stomach. Hamsun turns to Ersine. From the distracted look in the Kurd's black eyes, as if the girl on the foredeck is no more than a phantom, Hamsun guesses that Ersine saw them come aboard together. He feels he owes an explanation. But what? They have been together since Carpathos, yet he knows little about her, merely that she is someone without motives, plans or goals, without consciousness of self. Why she attached herself to him, he can't say. They have little in common beyond a hunger to keep moving, see the next thing, be in the next place. Now she is with him; later it will be someone else. He won't let himself think about it. "A companion," he says. "Someone I met."

Ersine grasps Hamsun's arm and leans close. "You are man of world," he says solemnly. "You are professor, I am thinking."

Hamsun shakes his head, puzzled. "No, you're wrong. I've knocked around a little, nothing more."

Ersine's grip tightens. He's very strong, a man who has worked in the fields. He bends nearer, whispering: "You will be helping me, please. You will be giving me the good advise."

"Advice," Hamsun corrects.

The Kurd brightens. "You see, you are knowing many things."

They sit in the shade on a bench vacated by students, most of whom have climbed to the upper deck to enjoy the sun. Hamsun looks for the girl who was with the boy in the Hawaiian shirt, but she isn't around. Ersine orders tea and, when the boy arrives with two steaming glasses, won't allow Hamsun to pay. "You are guest in my country. You must not to be paying."

Ersine, it turns out, is in love. She is gentle, clever and beautiful beyond description, a pious young woman from Diyarbakir. "She is properly covering the self—not like shameful city girls." His voice is pitched low, his dark eyes focused on the pale moon of Hamsun's face. He has known the girl since childhood and loved her since he was old enough to understand the word. She is from a good family, neighbors owning farmland bordering Ersine's fields. She is perfection. "There is being no other woman for me. All my days I am waiting only to be marrying with Yesim." He caresses her name, adding syllables, drawing them out: "*Ye sss sheem.*"

Hamsun is pleased for the Kurd. It is good to hear someone speak of another with such tenderness. He sees the course of Ersine's life: he will live piously with the woman he loves; she will bear many children; they will live an old age of contentment and die fulfilled. He shakes off a pang of envy. "You're very lucky," he says.

"No," Ersine says. "Not being true."

"What do you mean?"

"She is not loving me."

Yesim is a student at the national university in Istanbul, a second year honor's scholar in the faculty of law. Ersine visited the city, hoping to speak with her, but she refused to see him.

"Is there another man?"

From the look of astonishment on Ersine's face, Hamsun might have asked if the beautiful and chaste law student were a space alien.

"Such a thing is not being possible. There is only Ersine loving Yesim."

"You're sure?"

Ersine rolls his eyes skyward. Hamsun's question doesn't deserve an answer.

"If there isn't another man, what can I tell you?"

"How to change her, please." Ersine's face is still, his dark gaze reading the pale wash of Hamsun's eyes. "What must I do to make her love me?"

They pass a small island, a rock really, with a navigational light blinking above it. Soon there is another, larger island, then a third with villas perched among gardens on a hillside. Students gather their things and move toward the railing.

Now Hamsun's certain Ersine saw him come aboard with Robin. That's why he sought him out. If Robin travels with Hamsun, she must love him. And if this is true, Hamsun must have some knowledge, some worldly wisdom beyond the ken of Diyarbakir.

He explains to Ersine that he must be kind to Yesim. He must be patient and give her time. He must not pressure her. "If she is to love you, she must come to it by herself. If not, you must look for someone else. If I were you I'd begin looking now."

Ersine throws back his head, teeth flashing as he laughs. "You will be seeing. I marry with her anyway, if she is loving me or not."

"And if she says no?"

"It makes no difference. It is arranged."

They fall silent and Hamsun slips away to the railing. The ferry from Kabatas sails across a broad bay and docks at one of the Princes' Islands. The students file down the gangway, laughing and singing as they cakewalk across the quay toward a village where tile-roofed buildings line narrow streets. It's hot, and in the hills above the village steam rises from scarlet bougainvillaea growing thickly around walled villas. When the gangway is raised and the ship, its propeller churning sand from the shallow bottom, backs from the quay, reverses, and begins its run toward the open sea, Hamsun watches the island drop astern. Then he lies down on a bench in the shade and falls into a doze.

It's afternoon when he wakes. The sea is choppy and in the

distance, beyond the coastal plane, thunderheads billow above steep mountains. A sharp wind blows down from the heights. He lies still for a while, his body rolling stiffly from side to side as the ship wallows in the chop. He checks his watch. Nearly five o'clock. Getting to his feet, he finds his way to the stairs. The ship is almost deserted. In the lounge off-duty seamen play cards at a corner table and the teaboy is asleep behind the bar. Hamsun wakes him and the boy makes coffee hot and thick as lava. Hamsun has taken only a sip when Ersine mounts the stool beside him and offers a Maltepe.

"We will smoke," Ersine says. "Then I will explain."

Hamsun waves a hand as if discarding something. "No need." He is already in Yalova, finding his bus on a dusty back street, climbing the steps and settling into a seat, setting out for Urgup. Like so much else, Ersine is behind him, Ersine and the ferry from Kabatas.

"But you are angry with me. This makes for sadness."

"Not angry," Hamsun says. "I don't understand, that's all. How you can marry someone who doesn't love you. Someone who has no choice."

"Yesim is not only person not having choice. I, too, must marry with her, even if I am not loving her. It is arranged when we are small. Her family is saying, 'Ersine, you must get education and job with government, then you will be marrying with our Yesim.' My father is agreeing. These things I have done."

"And Yesim?"

"Is finishing with faculty of law, then coming to Diyarbakir to be marrying."

"And she'll practice her profession?"

"Ersine is having two tractors and many hectares, employment in Ministry of Posts. The woman of Ersine is not working."

Hamsun orders more coffee and they sit smoking. The seamen lay down their cards and go on deck to ready the ship for landing. The teaboy vanishes and only Hamsun and Ersine are left in the lounge. Beyond the windows Yalova is visible—minarets, the dock, a row of low buildings, the mountains behind.

"There's still something I don't understand," Hamsun says.

"Yes?"

"If it makes no difference, why did you ask how to change her?"

Ersine looks into Hamsun's face and smiles. "Ah, my friend, if Yesim would be loving me, it would make for much happiness. I would be—how you say?—in heaven."

Standing at the railing as the ship left the Princes' Island, Hamsun had seen the boy in the Hawaiian shirt, the girl beside him, her arm slung brazenly around his waist as they turned into a side street. Not far away, rucksack slanted above her shoulders, Robin peered into a shop window, her golden hair and skimpy costume unmistakable in the sunlight. The place must have appealed to her. The posh villas on the hillsides, the sandy beaches along the bay.

"Yes," he says, feeling a bump as the ship nudges the quay. "That's how we say—in heaven."

Hawsers go ashore, the gangway rattles down. Hamsun and Ersine sit side-by-side as if waiting for the ship to begin its return voyage. Finally, Ersine swings from his stool. Hamsun joins him and they pass through the empty lounge, along a companionway and up the stairs to the main deck.

COMIC VALENTINE

Rain. Tugging a pillow over frizzed hair, Miriam Simmons tries to shut out the roar. Rain—for days, weeks, even. No one remembers how long. Miriam crams the pillow down tight, longing to sleep another hour. Two hours. Deep sleep. All the way under.

Instead, she listens to her husband Ray using the toilet, showering, shaving, brushing his teeth. An Aquarius, all his sounds are water sounds. If he isn't dripping on the Flockati carpet following an afternoon sail, he's pouring sweat from too much tennis. Day or night there's a drink in his hand. "Reestablishing my fluid balance," he says, a small blue eye winking in his heavy face. Usually, it's gin. Sometimes, Scotch. Bourbon, if handy. "Bourbon and branch," he says grinning, digging an elbow into his host's ribs. He reminds Miriam of Haydn's "Water Music." Or was it Handel? How can anyone remember at such an ungodly hour on a sopping morning?

Miriam has a problem. Which is uncommon up here. Up here

people have relationships and life-styles. They have affairs. They have silver BMW roadsters and Jacuzzis and lap pools and pedigreed dogs with sterling choke-chains. They have Mexican women named Inez or Esther or Carlotta to do the cleaning and cooking, to look after the kids. They have lifetime memberships to Bodyfirm and the Coral Casino.

They have time.

They do not have problems. A problem is something Miriam's daughter Charlotte would have in her mathematics class, if she had a mathematics class. Charlotte attends the Frascati School. She has golden hair, a pierced brow studded with silver, and a boyfriend with a Harley chopper.

Charlotte is not Miriam's problem.

At less exalted altitudes, down in the world of nine-to-five, Miriam's problem would be the usual one. Her neighbors would notice, then forget it.

Not so up here. Up here, it's a topic of gossip. No one understands how she can let her problem interfere with the afternoon shop at the Village Mart. It's here, after tennis and before picking up kids from orthodontists, equitation, Chi Kung, the women hover near the delicatessen, gripping their shopping carts and talking about it.

"Oh, sure," Caroline Carver says, brushing perfectly frosted hair from Maybellined eyes, "One of us might drink a glass of chilled Chablis with lunch but that's the end of it, right there!"

"At least until cocktail time," Becky Smollet adds, eyeing the jug of sherry in her cart.

Maybe Miriam has the problem just to keep from coming here. No one thinks of that. She saw a movie once on late-night TV: *The Stepford Wives*. She knows the look: tennis dresses white as Alps, glossed lips and nail varnish a pale coral, shopping carts bearing daily rations of raspberries and tenderloins, *Bain de Soleil*, Q-Tips and Massengill's Disposable Douche. Most of all she knows the suntans. The bronzed depilated legs, cordovan shoulders, faces rich as carved mahogany.

Miriam sees little of the sun, herself. Her days are spent in dimness. Standing before a full-length mirror, hot water sizzling into the tub, she sees no bikini line. Top to bottom her body has the terrible pallor of a blank page of writing paper.

In an earlier century they would have found her perfect.

For all the good that does.

The refrigerator light winks on. Miriam peers inside. Everything is there: *babaghanouji, avgolemono*, soya milk, blue-corn tortillas, *raddichio* in the crisper. Miriam's Coalport platter bears a leftover slab of Claude Lavore's jellied veal mousse. Beside it, a crock of Stilton and a jar of Dundee marmalade. Miriam's problem is in here, too. She doesn't need to look further. She knows exactly where to go. After filling a tumbler half and half with orange juice and vodka, she leans against the counter, holding the icy glass against her sheer apricot nightgown. It burns like fire. This is it, she thinks. The first drink of the day.

Down at AA they tell you to take your life one day at a time. Miriam's never heard them say this but she knows they do. They hold their meetings in the basement of a neighborhood church. Chain-smoke cigarettes, drink cup after cup of powerful black coffee and tell the sordid stories of their lives. Miriam has never set foot in the basement, never heard the organ groaning overhead. The sordid stories have escaped her, yet she knows they're true.

If it wasn't for her problem she has a strong feeling she'd have nothing at all.

She tosses off the drink, then pours another which she carries to the breakfast alcove where she slides into the leatherette booth. Rain streams down the windows. Beyond the glass she makes out the sodden shapes of trees and bushes bent under a burden of water. A fish tank, she thinks. A goddamn fish tank. She doesn't know the name of a single green thing growing out there. Next spring she'll walk through the yard with her gardener, have him explain what these things are called. She's threatened to do this for years. Never has. This year she'll fool everyone and go through with it. She is resolved.

Bravo!

She toasts her decision, then holds the glass to the watery light. A golden color filters through. At his very moment every woman within a radius of a dozen miles is down at Skin Deep Tanning Studios on Village Ridge Road. She sees them lined up in identical tinfoil coffins, thousands of watts of sunlamps trained on their naked hides, their soft little nipples smeared with cocoa butter; wads of dampened cotton bandage blue-lidded eyes. Yanni's *jejune arpeggios* filter in ad nauseam. Soft-voiced gossip traded from tomb to tomb.

She's had three or four. Maybe five. In any event she's had a few and will have another. Thank you very much!

Prost. Ziveli. Cin-cin.

She makes a cup of instant coffee which she manages to consume, and toast which she doesn't. It lies cold on the counter top, butter smeared crudely on charred edges.

"*Zivio!*"

She remembers that one from their cruise down the Dalmatian coast. The year Charlotte sulked all summer because she missed Stark Naked and the Sex Merchants' American tour. And Miriam and Raymond Simmons sat on deck, watching the ghostly coast slip past, drinking glass after glass of plum brandy, hoping somehow to lessen the terrible weight of unhappiness that plagued their only child.

It was awful. Just plain awful.

Miriam finishes her drink and makes another. Suddenly,

there's loud noise in the dining room, a nervous, high-pitched roar like a jet in a holding pattern. Clinging to her drink she lurches through the swinging door. In a red uniform, pink rag tied around inky hair, Inez or Esther or Carlotta runs the Hoover over a carpet the color of old wine. She concentrates as she pushes the chromium machine across the room, banging into chairs and the carved legs of tables. Why do they let these people into the country? They're a menace. Can't speak the language. The woman's name, Miriam knows full well, is Mary Carrillo. She was born and lives in her family home hardly a mile away. Bilingual, she speaks English without an accent. She comes from an extensive, close-knit clan where cousins, uncles, sisters and brothers perform tasks some people deem essential. They build roads, cut the grass, make Miriam's deposits at the bank. Mary Carrillo's son Jorge studies law at Stanford. Miriam watches Mary Carrillo run the vacuum over the floor, dust sucked into the machine from the dark carpet, the golden *fleurs-de-lis*.

From where she waits in the silver Mercedes, Miriam listens to the downpour, the rush of water down Las Cruces Canyon. Normally there's just a trickle. This afternoon, as shoppers splash across the parking lot into the Village Mart, the creek roars past below Hair Spectrum and Operation Petticoat. It sounds like Mary Carrillo piloting the Hoover. It sounds like disaster.

Her husband slides in beside her. She doesn't turn to look but visualizes water dripping from the brim of his hat, puddling under heavy brown shoes. Starting the car, he circles once around the green, waving to passing cars. There are the Christensens, the Finamores, Steins and Moolmans. There are the Carvers and Strongs.

Out on the road he asks Miriam about her day. His wet, throaty voice accompanies the slap of the wipers, the hiss of water under the tires. He doesn't expect a response and she doesn't give one. Is she expected to tell him she's been drunk twice and slept it off? Is she to say that Mary Carrillo broke the Claude Lavore coffee carafe? That Charlotte rode home on the back of her boyfriend's Harley? That she came in soaked and muddy, took a hot bath and went straight to bed without speaking? Forget it. He doesn't want to know.

Instead, mechanically, she turns the question on him.

"Oh, the usual." He looks at her, grinning, his face a full moon in the failing light. "You know how it is, tampering with the delicate plumbing of some of our more notorious maidens."

Ray Simmons is a gynecologist. He gives Miriam the answer he always gives when laymen ask about his work. He thinks it funny. He actually laughs.

Miriam doesn't think it funny. She doesn't laugh. "No," she says, "as a matter of fact, I don't know how it is. You'll have to tell me sometime, Raymond. But not tonight. I don't think I could stand it tonight."

Ray has other things to say about his work, but saves it for locker rooms and sailing friends: "Being an OB-GYNer is a whole lot like being a hotel detective—I'm always down on my knees, peeking through keyholes."

This one Miriam overhears from time to time, wondering when she does why she married this man. Just as she wonders on nights they're both sober enough and he reaches for her in the dark.

They're all here. You can tell by the BMWs, the Mercedes and SUVs slotted into the clubhouse lot. Hal Sawyer's red Ferrari with its Swiss license plates is out there too, gleaming under a steady downpour. And P.Y. Hsu's Morgan roadster, its royal racing green coachwork sinking into the deeper greens of the sodden forest.

Inside, they're three and four deep at the bar: the Christensens, Wonders, the Hardwick Drakes and a few dozen others joking, laughing, toasting this and that. At one end of the bar Ray Simmons swaps sailing yarns with Brewster St. John. On a stool at the other end Miriam stares into her third martini.

It's been served on the stem, two short cellophane straws slanted against the rim of the glass. A green olive lies beneath two inches of icy Beefeaters, sans toothpick. Miriam feels she must eat the olive. She needs the nourishment. She hasn't eaten anything since a slice of cold toast at mid-afternoon. The trouble is, she can't figure out how to retrieve the olive from the glass. The straws baffle her. Would anyone drink a martini through straws? On the other hand, why are they there? Is she expected to manipulate them like chopsticks to draw the olive out? Impossible. It would take more dexterity than she can even imagine. Bemused, she stares into her glass.

Hal Sawyer suddenly appears at her shoulder, big, tanned, graying. Ice-blue eyes, hawk nose and a broad mouth tell her he's capable of handling anything. Taking the glass from her hand he spears the olive with a straw and holds it like a lollipop before her grateful lips. She slowly chews the gin-soaked fruit. Hal Sawyer and Miriam Simmons smile into one another's eyes.

Later, they dance. A combo—electric bass, saxophone, piano, drums—plays slow ones and fast ones. Hal and Miriam dance the slow ones, not bothering to talk, Hal's chin resting on Miriam's hair. During the fast ones they pass the buffet tables with their smoked salmons, salads and prime ribs of beef, then join the crowd at the bar. Miriam orders another martini; Hal, vodka on ice.

This club's not special. They all belong to more elegant ones. But it's here they come to relax. It has a pool and tennis courts, a sauna and massage rooms. The clubhouse itself is low and modern, built of redwood and glass, its cantilevered deck suspended above a bend in the boulder strewn creek.

Tonight, the bend has vanished, replaced by a steadily rising flow of debris-laden water pouring from the forest, boiling in brown rapids just inches beneath the deck before vanishing into the blackness of the rainy night. Already a tennis court has been cut away. One net post still stands while the other dangles in the widening canyon. The net is taut between them as if modern man has relearned some primitive way to fish, is learning to survive beyond the Apocalypse.

Actually, no one cares about the Apocalypse. Not with booze to think about—booze and food, the slow ones to dance to and the fooling around with other men's wives, other women's husbands.

Though, if Hal Sawyer knew that at this very instant the front wheel of his Ferrari was dropping into a hole opened in the pavement by the rising stream and water was creeping toward twelve perfect cylinders, twelve perfectly tuned carburetors, he'd undoubtedly move his automobile to higher ground.

But he's preoccupied. You can't blame him. He has his vodka on ice and Miriam Simmons' thigh riding against his own and the band sliding into "My Funny Valentine." He has a burning sensation deep in his pants that might be prostate trouble rather than desire.

Taking Miriam in his arms, Hal slides into a slow foxtrot.

Is your figure less than Greek
Is your mouth a little weak
When you open it to speak
are you . . . ?

At the bar Ray Simmons tells Brewster St. John that being an OB-GYNer is like being a hotel detective while Marjorie Moolman weeps into Eric Strong's collar.

On the dance floor Hal clasps Miriam and smells her hair. She tucks her face into his shoulder, feeling her limbs melting.

Stay little Valentine, staaaa-ay
Each day is Valentine's daaaa-ay!

Hal opens a door and the two slip onto the terrace. Rain pummels the roofing overhead as water sweeps darkly beneath the deck. The foundations groan as if an old house were settling into a state of ultimate repose. Like survivors adrift on a midnight river, Hal and Miriam cling to one another. The deck quakes beneath them. No pretense of dancing now. It's body against body as rain whips around them on a sudden wind. Something in the way Miriam took the olive between fuchsia lips makes Hal long to kiss her. In a minute he will. First he will hold her, smell her hair, steady himself so that at the crucial moment he won't fall. Later, across the back seat of someone's sedan . . . .

"I'm so happy," Miriam says. "So happy I could die."

"What?" Hal asks. "What did you say?"

Miriam's head lolls; her eyes blur. "I'm so happy," she whispers, "sooo-o happy."

Beyond Hal's well-tailored shoulder, a shape appears in the lighted doorway. A large, lumpy, wet shape. The shape of Ray Simmons.

"What's going on out here?"

Hal, groping for Miriam's mouth with his own, goes rigid.

"Don't fight over me," Miriam says. "I'm not worth it."

Neither man listens.

"Look, Hal, you'd better check on your goddamn car," Ray says, grasping a glass in his wet hand. "Parking lot's given way on that side—whole thing washed into the drink. Your goddamn car's half-way to Mussel Shoals by now."

Miriam watches Hal push past the shape in the doorway and vanish into the lighted room. Alone, she listens to the roaring creek. The deck shudders. "I was soooo-o happy," she says, "soooo-o happy I wanted . . . ."

"All right, Miriam, that's enough." The dark shape makes no effort to come to her. "Get inside, pick up your things. We're starting home before it's too goddamn late."

Turning from her husband Miriam steps from under the canopy and sways to the brink of the deck. Instantly, she's soaked through. Her *crepe de Chine* cocktail dress clings more closely than Hal Sawyer ever did. The deck shudders. There's a terrific shrieking as if a thousand nails were torn from a thousand planks, though louder, louder even than the rain, louder than the midnight river. The deck plunges, heaves upward, plunges again. Water races over the tops of Miriam's Ferragamo shoes as her eyes dart to Ray. Faces press around him in the lighted door. There's Caroline Carver, and P.Y. Hsu standing on a chair. Arms wave in alarm. Miriam doesn't move. What's the point? She was so happy she could have died. Now she can't remember why. Gripping the rail she holds on tight. The deck pitches. A hollow crump, a sudden sickening slide as it wrenches from the building. Miriam aboard, it drops into the flood.

"Miriam, goddamn!"

No reply.

She's spotted once, moments later, passing through the glow of arc lights beamed on the vanished tennis court. She strokes once, twice, three times, then turns to wave. Her face is radiant. She's outward bound.

Charlie Carrillo, Mary's grave, handsome cousin, sways in the saddle, a hand lifted against the glare of morning sun; the soil is dark as coffee from last night's storm. Charlie's big palomino Chongo picks his way through chaparral along the shoulder of Las Cruces Ridge. Man and horse move downhill, shale chattering under Chongo's hooves. Charlie braces his boots in the stirrups and lifts the reins. Far behind him he hears the other horses clattering through brush. That's Modoc, he thinks. Modoc and Amigo. They're okay on a bridle path but not much good up here anymore. They'll say that about Charlie Carrillo soon enough, he thinks, lifting his hat to brush a hand across graying hair. But not yet. There's a ride or two left before they haul him around on a mattress in the bed of a pickup. "Hup, Chongo," he says as much to hear the sound of a voice as to encourage his horse. "Hup, Chongo."

Then he spots her, a speck of whitish-pink among sycamore and scrub oak far down the slope. He knows without question it's Miriam Simmons. He's seen her many times when he's come to pick up Mary from work. He'd recognize her anywhere. Even fifteen feet up a sycamore, stark naked.

Still, he must be certain. That's one of the rules. Dismounting, he loops Chongo's reins over a sumac branch and unslings his Army surplus field glasses from the saddle horn.

He sits on a sun-warmed boulder, toying with a twig when the others arrive, their horses breaking from the chaparral into the clearing. Charlie doesn't move. "Found her," he says, without looking up.

"Where?" they ask.

Charlie says nothing. Rising, he swings onto his horse. "Ride up the ridge," he tells them. "Have the Forestry radio Search and Rescue and telephone her husband. If he takes the path where Riven Rock dead-ends, he'll find her a hundred yards down-stream. Make sure he brings a blanket and goes in first, that he's followed up close by a hook-and-ladder crew and paramedics. Me and Chongo'll ride down from here."

"She okay?" Johnny Ruiz asks. "You want me to ride in with you?"

"Wet and cold," Charlie says. "The poor woman is wet and cold. What'd you expect after a night like she's had. Otherwise, she looks okay. She's moving. She's alive." He wheels his horse and starts down the steep shale-spill slope.

*   *   *

Ray Simmons isn't used to this. Tennis courts and golf courses, yes. An occasional game of racquetball or a few laps in the pool. But, not this. Hiking over rough country is bad enough, but the silt, rubble and mud, the twisted branches and boulders flung against tree trunks make the going nearly impossible. Sweat beads on his forehead, drips deep in his armpits. Still and all, he's got to do it. Miriam is somewhere just ahead. After a night riding in sheriffs' cars, waiting for word of discovery, he can hardly believe she's been found. Alive! That's what really gets him. Somehow, she managed to survive. And they're already calling her by a new name: Missus Swimming-Simmons! Just when he was getting used to the idea she'd drowned in the night.

He spies the horse first: Chongo browsing on scrub, a line on his neck, saddle and bridle slung over the trunk of a fallen tree. And Charlie Carrillo, hat pushed back on his tanned face, thumbs hooked into a silver-studded belt.

"It's good you brought the blanket," Charlie says. "She'll need it." He jerks a thumb over his shoulder. "She's through there. Keep your eyes up. Watch the ground and you'll miss her. Get her covered and I'll bring the rest on down."

Ray Simmons hears the paramedics on the trail behind him, the men with the ladder. He ducks past Charlie and pushes through the brush. The muddy ground sucks at his shoes. The bright February sky is blotted out by enormous oaks. *Why me?* he wonders, trying not to slip in the muck. Why do I have to go in first? Why hasn't she been helicoptered out of here and wheeled into a crisp white hospital room? That's the way it happens on TV. He's seen it dozens of times. But, somehow, just as you'd expect with Miriam, something's gone wrong. She just can't do anything in the normal way. Always the oddball. Though, he supposes, he should be pleased she managed to save herself. But there is this name business: Missus Swimming-Simmons.

—63—

He'll spend the rest of his life living that one down.

"Miriam," he calls, "you didn't follow instructions. If you'd followed instructions we wouldn't be in this mess. We'd have spent the night in our own bed. I'd be at my office right now—where I belong. You'd be home looking after things. The basement's flooded. Charlotte's down with flu."

Miriam envisions her husband as one of those pamphlets that come with new appliances: Your Kitchen Range—Some Do's and Don'ts. "Do come inside. Don't stand in the rain. Do start for home while the car is on dry land." She wonders if he treats his patients this way, those "notorious maidens" of whom he's so enamored. Of course, he does. "Do step out of your clothing. Do . . . ."

Crouched on the limb of this tree forever and ever. Cold so long she's forgotten what warm is. The tree's become home. A refuge. Clinging to the limb while the flood waters surged around her, she felt her clothes drawn from her as if by the hands of a lover. Only now, perched in a swath of sunlight, her husband below, is she aware of her nakedness. From his vantage, Ray has the view of a hotel detective when he's down on his knees. She covers herself. Like Eve, she thinks, she might pluck a leaf from this tree.

"I'll toss the blanket up," Ray hollers. "Wrap yourself in it."

The blanket sails her way. She makes no effort to catch it. No effort at all. In the distance she hears the others coming. Eyes peer from the underbrush.

"Miriam!" the doctor shouts. "Goddamn it, will you co-operate?"

Again, the blanket ascends, rises to within an arm's length. She doesn't notice. Faces draw near as the sun drifts overhead. Missus Swimming-Simmons starts upward, reaching for a branch. High overhead.

PARADE'S END

"The Yermo Lounge?" he asked.

The Chevy pulled out of the Wanderlust Motel and turned toward town.

"Taking me back where you found me?"

"Any better ideas?"

They hadn't talked about it. Hadn't talked about anything. After she found him asleep in the Chevy, Fern waited, sitting inside the stale room, hands folded, suddenly calm, watching. The sun broke over the roof's edge and through the windshield, waking him. Unfolding himself from behind the wheel, he walked in, rumpled and truculent: "Came for my stuff."

She didn't move, knew only that it was over. Richie crossed to the bathroom and turned. "You okay?"

Then he was gone. Through the partially open door she heard his clothes drop to the floor, the sudden hissing of the shower. She waited for the sound of his voice above the spray. The shower ceased abruptly, and she heard the rusty working of the toilet.

Wrapped in a towel, Richie emerged and began dressing. He

didn't bother turning, nor did Fern look away. Yet there was no familiarity. Suddenly they were strangers. When he pulled on the fresh clothes she'd laid out for him, he smoothed his hair and stepped to the dresser.

Fern caught his glance in the mirror, blank, blue eyes cool and distant. Nothing she could do to change that. He took her key from among the clutter of cosmetics and left without speaking.

She had packed his two bags by the time he came back. Her own things still scattered over the room. "You check out?" she asked.

"Paid up . . . and a couple of days in advance. Told the old lady you'd probably stay through Wednesday. Don't know your plans, but should give you time to figure something out."

"Such concern."

"Don't want any hassles, that's all."

"Won't get any from me—I was taught to be accommodating."

They stood in silence. Richie glanced at the open suitcase on the bed and the other near the door.

"Thanks for getting my stuff ready."

"Gave me something to do."

"Uh-huh."

"Wait," she said, "I'm still wearing your robe."

He leaned against the door, hands behind him, resting on the knob. "Doesn't matter. Keep it. I can pick up another."

Fern's fingers were already busy at the tie. He watched her slip off the robe, folding it into his suitcase.

"If you want a lift into town," he said, "get dressed. I'm going that way."

They rode toward Farnum in silence. The midmorning sun slanted across the fields, the black smear of highway. Doves veered in clusters above stands of blood-red flax. Despite the Labor Day holiday, a solitary tractor groaned along the rim of an irrigation canal. The Chevy sped past an empty gin yard, then the gin itself, its high metallic walls shimmering in the heat. At last they reached the gas stations and truck parks at the junction where Highway 86 bore south. Traffic was sparse. Richie slipped the intersection on the yellow and sped straight up Main Street.

As they approached the town plaza, Fern heard music: a blare of brass, the steady throbbing of a drum. Her head ached; the glare stabbed her eyes. In her hurry, she'd forgotten her sunglasses. Her purse was back at the motel. Clutching cigarettes and lighter, she cursed the heat. On their right they passed the shady façade of the Plantation House looming behind palms. She wondered if her old beau Art Driscol still perched there in the dimness, hidden behind his martinis, but knew she didn't care. Ahead lay the plaza, a green-fringed park surrounding tile-roofed civic buildings. Main Street bore right, a zebra-striped traffic barrier angled across it. Richie swerved around the barrier and gunned ahead.

"You sure you can . . ."

"Doesn't matter . . . told you I'd get you downtown."

Passing the hotel, they reached the place where Picacho Road entered from the south. They encountered people crowding the street. Massed in worn khaki beneath an array of straw hats, farm laborers enjoyed the holiday. School kids shouted, dashing among khaki legs or rolled by on bicycles hung with paper streamers. A police car was parked broadside across the road, but no policemen around. Beating the horn, Richie pulled past it, edging into the crowd.

"Mexicans," he said with sudden rage. "Must be these union guys on strike'"

Slanting a hand above her eyes, Fern watched as the line of men abruptly parted. Ahead she caught a glimpse of something silver, heard the sharp, papery rattle of drums as the Chevy shot through.

"Look, I tried to tell you . . ."

"What the . . . Jesus! Look out on your side!"

"Maybe you can still back up."

Slamming to a stop, Richie jammed the car into reverse. Too late. The crowd closed in behind. Ahead, drenched in silver-studded leather, their riders decked-out in fringed buckskin of green and gold, thirty matched palominos jangled over shimmering asphalt. Farnum's Labor Day parade bore down on them: a National Guard platoon raggedly quickstepping behind massed flags, a high school marching band swinging "Dixie," the Elks Club float overflowing with crepe paper, bathing beauties and a purple chow dog bearing a tinfoil crown. Beyond more horses, bands and a cop cruising closer on a Harley-Davidson.

"Jesus Christ! Can you believe this?"

"You'll have to go ahead now."

"Shiiiit! Goddamn! You think I don't know?"

"Look, it won't do any good to . . ."

"Shut up!" Richie's fist slammed the dashboard. The car jerked forward. Wedged between Company B of the 192nd Engineers Battalion of the National Guard and the massed dove-colored rumps of the Pauma Valley Mounted Sheriff's Posse, they crept around the plaza and swung up Main Street. On the arcaded sidewalks, townspeople gazed into the heat shimmer and fumes to witness the passing pageant.

"Why don't you relax? It's only two more blocks.".

Richie slumped behind the steering wheel. "Thanks, I'll make a point of counting them." He turned aside to hawk through the open window. "One thing you have to say for these hick towns," he went on, looking sourly ahead, "they sure are hounds for parades."

Despite her fatigue and the headache that rose along her spine and pounded her skull, Fern found herself laughing. At first quietly, then as the ludicrousness of their situation dawned, her laughter rose in shrill peals, joining wildly with the bands, hoof clatter and jangling tack. She wept. She pounded the seat, her face split with hysteria.

Richie glared. "Why don't you shut the fuck up!"

"Don't you see?" she gasped. "The parade . . . ." Again laughter took over. A joyless, uncontrollable gush rolling on until Richie reached across and struck her hard across the mouth.

"Okay," she said, suddenly sensible, sensible perhaps for the first time since she'd met him. "That's it."

Her lip began to swell.

They entered the second block. Leaning forward, Fern made out the Yermo Lounge, its pink scaling façade. The sun beat against crumbling stucco as if, at any moment, it would transform it into pure dazzling light. The parade crawled forward, palominos prancing dizzily ahead, the troop of bored soldiers, rifles slung at their shoulders, pressing behind. Under the arcades the crowd gawked and cheered, wondering, undoubtedly, how this strange, gloomy couple in the red Chevy Caprice happened into the spectacle. Fern wondered too, wondered at the folly of her life. Licking her lip, she tasted the faint, sweet flavor of blood.

"This is far enough," she said calmly. "Let me out right here."

They went on. Richie turned to her, his face turbulent and strained. "Told you I'd take you . . . ."

They argued, the parade's blare drowning their voices as the morning's silence spilled into rancor. The car jerked forward. They shouted unintelligible words, noise beating against Fern's ears: the dissonance of Richie's anger, her own venomous phrases. Neither heard the other. It made no difference. It was over. Fern was void of everything but the heated words. They were nothing more than a final waving of the flag of defeat. Had there ever been anything worth winning? Looking toward Richie, flushed and angry as he cramped the car into the curb, it didn't seem so. When they lurched to a stop, she opened the door and stepped out.

At the curb, she turned back, the crowd pressing around her, sweaty and oppressive. On his side, Richie, too, was out, leaning over the car's roof, his arms flung across the grimy red paint. Beyond him, paraders slogged through the heat: an all-girl drill team now, batons flashing. Fern strained forward, caught his voice lifting over the din:

"Hey, wait! What'd you expect?"

"What?"

The cop on the Harley reached him, urging him to move the car. Another policeman approached on foot. Raising his voice, Richie ignored them both.

"What do you want?"

"Look, I can't . . ."

"A house in the suburbs, for Christ's sake? Kids and dogs and toys and crappy diapers?"

"What? No. No, nothing like . . ."

"Jesus, can't you see? That's what I've been running from all my life.

The cop laid a hand on Richie's arm. Fern spun away, pushing through the crowd. She, too, was running. Running.

WING WALKING

Louisville, via Roseland to Peru

Weddings weren't important to Marta, not like they were to
her girlfriends. From the time they were given their first bra and
panty sets and sniffed the heady fragrance of their first gardenia
corsages, they clipped pictures from *Bride and Groom*, stylish
bridal gowns, dress patterns, lushly colored ads for diamond
solitaires, then pasted them into albums mapped with throbbing
hearts. Marta's first wedding wasn't even celebrated in the candlelit nave of Louisville's Christ Church Cathedral, followed by
flung rice, cans tied to the wedding car, a horn-blaring parade up
Second Street to the Monument to the Confederate Dead. Nor
did she marry one of her crew-cut beaus with hip flasks and hot
cars who had whisked her off to sockhops under crepe paper
garlands in Central High's gym, followed by long sultry hours
parked beneath a Southern moon.

The nuptial knot was tied in the chambers of the Domestic
Relations Court for the Borough of Manhattan, City of New
York. Sheathed in an off-the-shoulder cocktail dress of Nile blue

taffeta, draped in the imitation leopard coat she bought the summer she made the Greyhound trip north, Marta stepped into the wintry glare of Twenty-Second St. on the arm of a man slightly older and shorter than herself, a man with slicked-back blond hair, a quick smile of dubious warmth and eyes as pale and shifty as river ice.

The groom was the youngest son of a Tidewater tobacco-growing family, their plantation up the Rappahannock River near Port Royal. At any rate that was Lou Sinclair's claim. He drew word pictures for Marta of the columned house, steamboats, darkies on the levee, balls where gentlemen slipped on white gloves before taking a lady's hand in the quadrille. A world of Southern grace throbbing in Lou's cowboy imagination. If the vision was insane, the voice and demeanor were hardly less so. Through the languor of the "Old South," you clearly discerned the flat drawl and jointless slouch of west Texas.

Marta, weaned on the nuances of Southern speech, the sing-song of Appalachia, the liquid ramble of the Piedmont, should have pegged Lou for a charlatan from the start. But her ear failed her. Done up in a cream colored double-breasted suit and snowy dancing pumps, Lou flashed his cuffs, fluffed a nut-brown handkerchief and hummed a silky tune that Marta claimed "Shut my ears, turned my head and swept me clean off my feet."

Lou never revealed what fluke of circumstance brought him to Arthur Murray's Fifth Avenue Studio, where Marta, lucky to land a job as dance instructor, hoofed it to a tune of her own. From the instant he took her in his arms, twirling her across the floor in a sequence of dips, whirls and arabesques, it was obvious he'd already taken the course .

Their courtship was quick and torrid by the repressive standards of the time. Cinched into the satin and Lastex of semiformal dress, they made the rounds of restaurants, nightclubs and ballrooms. They ate at Sweet's, sipped *créme de menthe frappes* in the Knickerbocker Bar and spent long afternoons at Roseland, dancing *pasodobles* around the great floor. Returning to Marta's residence club in the back of taxis, Lou told risqué stories that intimated the joys awaiting Marta when she became his bride, then squeezed her hard when she tittered and flushed pink with affection. Taking his pale hand in her own, she slipped it into her blouse and let his easygoing manipulations tighten the spring of desire.

Such was the nature of their intimacy when the newlyweds stepped onto Twenty-second Street and turned toward Lexington Avenue. Marta clasped Lou's arm and pressed her breast against the sleeve of his jacket as he led her around the corner into a blast of winter wind. "Windiest damn corner in all New Yawk," he drawled, drawing her nearer, "An that's a verifiable fact."

After champagne cocktails at the Gramercy and dinner in an Armenian place farther down Lexington, they caught a cab to the Village and checked into the Duke Hotel.

"For our little hon-a-moon," Lou said as they rode hip to hip in the creaking elevator. The aged elevator "boy" gave him a look. Lou winked, turning to his bride. "So much more convenient than going outta town, don't you know."

When Lou finished with her, Marta stood at the window looking down into the stop-and-go of Sixth Avenue. Behind her the bridegroom slept, his steady breathing balm to the bride. Persuaded this was all a woman could desire, she dropped her orchid nightgown over her head and smoothed it against her body. Traffic thickened and thinned with the changing lights. The room, with its threadbare carpet and hooded lamp, held her resplendent because of the sudden sweet heave and thrust of love.

Poised on one of life's most beautiful plateaus, they'd have an apartment of their own—a place in one of the projects, maybe a two-bedroom near Carl Schurz Park where young marrieds were moving in with their furniture payments and dreams of mocha wall-to-wall. They would have nice things. Marta toured Macy's and Gimbel's. With growing shrewdness she fingered brocades, debated the features of Frigidaire and Electrolux. The apartment done, they could sublet and be free to travel. Lou, it seemed, knew people everywhere, had financial connections from Boston to the Coast, had plans for making "ver-ah big bucks!"

Two weeks later they heaved their bags aboard the elevator and sank toward the Duke's gloomy lobby. Two weeks among a tangle of delicatessen containers and graying sheets, Lou mounted in any number of what Marta considered preposterous postures, running himself in and out of her as if he'd discovered the secret of perpetual motion. "Down where I come from," he said in grinning reference to the land of salt draws west of the Pecos that he gleefully admitted was home, "down there they always owned old Lou Sinclair would hump a woodpile if he reckoned there was a snake in it." As if to prove his point, he threw himself on her as if she were a stack of firewood harboring an anaconda in heat.

Finally Lou buckled his pants and told her they were moving.

"Just like that?"

"Come on, woman, we can't lie around here huffin' and puffin' the rest of our damn lives. We got people to meet, places to see, money to pick off the damn trees."

"Usually," she began, trying to restrain her sarcasm, "I say usually when people move, they have someplace to move to."

Lou grinned. "Now come on, girl, you got a real treat coming. Lou's gonna show you the whole damn world!"

So they moved. Not into a two-bedroom near Carl Schurz Park but into a secondhand Hudson sedan that Lou piloted west through the Holland Tunnel and across the industrial shoals and reefs of New Jersey.

The journey west took what was left of their marriage, swallowed it as the land swallowed the car. Cornland. Wheatland. Grassland. Mountains. Marta didn't know the country was so big. It numbed her, sent her into herself for protection. She dreamed the journey while Lou gripped the wheel, squinting into the glare, rambling endlessly about the deals he would make, the *ver-ah big bucks* that would be theirs to spend when at last they arrived. He promised her a convertible, palm trees, a lifetime of sunbathing on white sand beside the Pacific: "Sand so white you got to wear dark glasses just so you don't go blind looking at it. Sky as blue as a Monday morning mood." Yet, like a mirage, arrival sped always just ahead. They spent days swinging north, south, then west again. Sometimes they stopped for weeks in out-of-the-way motor courts and cut-rate hotels waiting for money that eventually appeared, in smaller amounts than hoped for, from sources Lou never revealed.

For a time they settled in Lebanon, Illinois, renting a turn-of-the-century house on a shady back street. "Roostin' just like real folks." While Marta worked part-time behind the perfume counter at Provost's Five-and-Dime and haunted the bus station's magazine rack and the counter at the Tulip Queen as if she were a pining adolescent becalmed in the doldrums of middle-America, Lou drove the Hudson between Lebanon and East St. Louis, where he had connections in the meat-packing game. "Big bucks in the meat business," he claimed, adjusting his porkpie hat and winking at himself in the mirror. He'd given up white linen in favor of a navy blue suit, black shirt, a finger-thin tie of palest yellow. "All a man needs to do is dress sharp, know when to smile and be willing to cut a few throats," he said, settling into the car, "and he's a surefire millionaire." Left behind, Marta plunged into plans for redoing the house and making a trip to Louisville for a family visit, postponed both and instead had her hair cut, polished her nails and watched the spring come in with its false promises.

Escape finally arrived when Lou, face bloodied, stumbled into their bedroom.

"Get your ass in gear, darlin', the bus is about to leave!"

She switched on the bedside lamp. It was three a.m. "Oh, my God, just look."

"Cut the damn light!" He backhanded the lamp from the table, jerked open a closet door and began cramming a suitcase with clothes.

"You're in trouble."

"Sheee-it, woman, tell me something I don't already know. Now, will you haul ass?"

Dawn washed the street with pale light by the time their bags were stowed in the Hudson's trunk. Lou sprang into the passenger seat. "Let's hotfoot it!" The right side of his face was raw, the puffed flesh around his eye turning the color of oil on water.

"You drive—I'll tell you where to turn."

They took U.S. 50 east out of town.

"Keep her slow." Lou studied the highway behind them. "Don't go attracting attention by doin' something dumb."

Beyond Carlyle a road branched north toward Greenville and Vandalia. Lou nodded and Marta turned. A narrow bridge, trees and brush tangled in a web of pallid spring growth, dark water motionless in pools and ponds among stunted hills. Marta bore down on the accelerator and the Hudson raced across the countryside. Rounding a corner she saw a barn, a man on a tractor, cows knee-deep in mud.

"Whew-eee!" Lou hollered after a few miles. "We're gonna be all right now, you hear. In the clear and home free!"

She glanced at him. He still stared through the rear window, the tension high in his damaged face, a nerve jumping along his jawbone. "Now would you please tell me?" she began, then abruptly stopped, her words hanging in the air like frozen laundry. A pair of strange eyes stared at her in the rearview mirror—

empty eyes, large, dark and whorled as thumb prints on a booking sheet. Around them the faded ellipse of a child-woman's face dissolved into insignificance.

"This here is Laura, darlin'," Lou said, introducing the girl who had lain all this time beneath a blanket on the floor in back. "Isn't that a name you could dance to? Da-da is the face in the misty night; footsteps that you hear down the hall. Now, isn't that some sweet name?"

Marta looked again, dumbstruck. Dark eyes groped toward her, feeling their way with no sense of direction or depth of space. The strawberry mouth tried to smile.

"How-do, ma'am."

Until the girl spoke Marta believed that life was understandable. If you asked the right questions, right answers would follow. It was only a matter of time until you discovered how the world turned. But piloting the Hudson through a landscape more impossibly green than the car itself, she understood this was not true. Laura's dark eyes told her. So did the pale, ice eyes of her husband. Forces existed that Marta Sinclair would never fathom. Like an oyster masking a particle of sand, the best she could wish was to fabricate a polished surface, wear it like a choker clasped at the throat of her feelings, an emblem to warn the world she didn't give a damn whether she understood it or not.

Lou shot her a look. "You okay? You seem a little funny."

"If anything seems funny, I'd say it was you and your—whatever you want to call her—in the back seat."

"Laura? Nothing ree-motely funny about our Laura. She's about the most unfunny little person I ever met. And she's in a bad jam-up. I explained how me and you would help her out."

"I'll bet you did."

"There's folks down there in East St. Loo-ee, would you believe, don't care a damn for a person who tries to get ahead. A nice little girl like our Laura tries to earn a living and they drive

—77—

her clean off the streets. Ain't a bit fair. That's what I told 'em: You got to give a person a chance." He touched the puffed flesh at his eye. "See what it got me, a mouse big enough to eat me alive. Those boys and girls play tough. Would have chopped little Laura to pieces and fed her to the catfish if I hadn't rassled her into the car and brought her along."

"You're a real man of action, Lou."

"In this world, darlin', action is the name of the game. He who don't act, don't make it. That's Lou's motto: the man don't act is a gone man."

Maybe she knew less than the waif riding the backseat, but Marta caught the drift of Lou's speech—the drift if not the sense. There was no making sense of this. Was she nothing but a dance-hall floozy, a gun moll escaping with this pair of hapless desperadoes? What about her future? The stairway to the stars? Was she, after all her plans, just as hapless as this Texas pimp with his blond pompadour and little dope-fiend whore? Dizzied by her downward spiral, she blinked and the Hudson slued onto the shoulder. Gravel chattered in the fender wells. Let it go, she thought. Let it all go. A fence, a ditch rimmed by reeds offered themselves. A telephone pole swung into view. She shook the impulse and jerked the car back onto the asphalt. Lou hardly noticed, caught up in a rambling monologue, voice lifting in a euphoric aria, a rich and familiar paean to himself.

In the back, Dark Eyes lived in another world.

Holding the car on course, Marta wondered why this man had married her. The more obvious question, why she'd married him, was of no consequence. She ticked off several reasons, most attributable to the razzle-dazzle of New York and the blindness of inexperience. If she'd presented Lou to her family in the parlor back home, they'd have known something was hidden beneath the slicked hair, the white suit and dancing pumps. They'd have called him a "fancy man." She'd have scoffed and married him anyway. He did possess a certain quality that passed for charm, kept his shoes polished, nails buffed, smile cocked like a thug's pistol in the teeth of a crime. That this paragon of sophistication and Southern solicitude had turned his attention on homesick Marta was enough to win her heart. But why choose her? Granted, she was ripe fruit but he could have that for the picking. Whenever Lou's testosterone reached a prescribed level and the mood struck him, a wink, the triggered smile, a knee pressed against a thigh got him what he wanted. "Little darlin', you wouldn't mind if I loved you up a little?" "Just hurry and unhook me, will you, Honey?"

Marta could always find a job of some kind, enough to offer Lou a few dollars. Dark Eyes could do as much, find work in a field that, God knew, Lou understood—and he hadn't married her. What was the point? He had her anyway. Had them both. Respectability? Companionship? She gave up. Motives only confused things. She did know it was only a matter of time before she'd shake this man and move on. Over the past few months she'd begun to learn the limits of reality. She did what she could, no more. Now, she had to get through the day. "Okay," she said, "Which way do I go?"

They raced through Normal and Wenona, were riding between green ditches and plowed fields toward Peru when the car skipped a beat, issued a series of tubercular coughs, gave a snort and died. From behind the wheel Marta watched the afternoon sun slant off the bottle-green hood. Lou stared into his hands. Dark Eyes reclined in a state nearer a narcoleptic fit than real sleep.

Lou roused himself. "Looks like we run outta gas. We got a gallon can in back. I'll get us going quicker'n snake can spit."

Marta sighed, shaking her head. "You forgot—we filled the tank in Minonk. Gauge says it's better than half full."

"Oh, my God!" Dark Eyes lifted her head and gazed toward

tree-studded bluffs. "What'll we do?" she whimpered, tears tracking her colorless face.

"Shut up!" Lou snapped. "If there's one thing I can't stand—"

"—it's hearing a woman cry." Marta finished his sentence. "Well, boyo, where's my man of action now?"

"You too," he shouted. "Hush your damn mouth. Soon as I figure what's wrong, I'll have us back on the road."

"Maybe if you actually lifted the hood and looked at the motor."

"Wise-ass bitch!" Quick as a hummingbird, Lou backhanded her and bounded from the car, poking his head under the hood as Marta dabbed blood from her lip.

Dark Eyes peered over the top of the seat. "You shouldn't oughta provoke him." For the first time she entered the land of the living. "Lou's about the most sweetest natured man, long as he ain't provoked. But you provoke him, Lord, he can turn mean. He's about the most meanest man I ever saw once the provocation's on him. Here, you wanna use my hanky? Looks like your mouth's gonna swell fit to bust."

"Thanks. I'm pretty used to this. Don't forget, I married him."

The dark eyes turned inward, dumbfounded, then went absolutely blank. "Huh?

Lou slammed the hood and poked his head in the window. "Sorry."

"I know," Marta said. "I shouldn't have provoked you."

"You know what a damn temper I got. It's best you don't mess with me."

"Fine. I won't mess. Now, how about the car?"

"Darned if I can figure what's wrong. I'll hitch into Peru. Get a mechanic to come out and have a look."

"Louie," Dark Eyes whined from the back. "You hurry back now, hear? It's gettin' dark and you know I'm just scared to death of the dark. Parked out here in this old car. Why Lord,

Louie, I'd be just petrified."

"Try and keep her from climbing outta her skin," Lou told Marta. "I'll be back"

"—quicker'n a snake can spit. You told me before." Marta grimaced through puffed lips. "We'll be waiting, darlin'. We'll be sitting right here."

When Lou swung aboard an oil rigger's truck bound for Peru, Marta turned to Dark Eyes. "Why don't you lie down? I'll tuck that blanket round so you can sleep."

"You don't want me here, do you? Far as you're concerned, I'm just in the way." She sat propped in a corner like a Storybook doll, pale legs stretched across the seat, thumb stuck between strawberry lips. The yellow chemise covering the little of her that was covered exposed spindly arms and chest bones zippered between trifling breasts. Her eyes looked clipped from inked paper and pasted to her face. "A person learns quick when they're not wanted. You get a sixth sense about gettin' the heave-ho. No matter how folks try, they can't hide it when they want somebody out. I wouldn't of come along if I'd known about you. Far be it for me to come between a couple'a lovebirds like you and Lou. If it wasn't for me, he'd of loved you up good before hopping that truck. Don't think I don't know what it's like having a man like Lou—man hung like a horse. You'd be spraddled yet and him jacking it to you if it wasn't for me. I'm a burden to you, a goddamn cross you got to bear. Just give the word—I'll say 'So long, it's been good to know ya.'"

Marta now knew what Lou meant about keeping the girl from climbing out of her skin. It wasn't some clever figure of speech, one of his oddball Southernisms. He meant it. She was stuck on this godforsaken road with a real loony-bird. "You settle down and get comfy," she crooned as soothingly as a psychiatric nurse comforting a madman with an axe. "Lou'll be along before you know it, Laura. We want you with us, love having you along. Get some rest now and soon as Lou gets here we'll be on our way."

Dark Eyes' lips sucked into a rosebud smirk. "In this car? This car ain't going nowhere. You thought maybe I was sleeping but I heard that racket it made. Run again? This old car is a gone car and you know it. You're just waitin' for me to drop off, then you're gonna pack off to Peru and find Lou. I know you got a plan. I know you're waitin' your chance to leave me behind. Wouldn't be the first time. I been left in jam-ups so bad you'd have to be Houdini himself to get yourself out. I been . . . ." Suddenly her face went soft and rubbery and she started to cry. "Lord, I knew when Lou sent that picture postcard I shouldn't oughta come. I never could say 'no' to that man. He only hasta ask and I melt and ooze all over him like cream cheese on a warm afternoon. He touches me and I open up like a honky-tonk on Saturday night."

The blood rushed to Marta's face. Not from jealousy or embarrassment, but from the nakedness of Dark Eyes' vulnerability, the desperation that prompted such admissions. But she fathomed what the girl said, knew Lou possessed an uncanny insight into a woman's darker rhythms, into the waves on which she rode. Despite his selfishness, his self-admiration, the uses to which he put others, that would be difficult to give up, impossible to forget. Soon though, she would give it up. Now there were places she wanted him to take her, things she wanted to know. "What picture postcard?" she asked. "Where in the world did you come from?"

"Wink."

"Wink?"

"Texas—water-tower town in the no-trees-at-all country. Population a thousand. Odessa's the big town for shoppin' and movies. That's where I met Lou—Odessa. I wasn't more'n twelve and didn't hardly have tit one." As if hoisting great weights, she cupped her hands under her chest, heaving upward.

"Odessa," she said, lowering imaginary bosoms. "San Angelo. Pecos. El Paso. Everywhere you can think of, me and Lou was raisin' hell."

"Sure you were. What ended it?"

"You know how it is with Lou. Spots something he wants and you and wild mustangs can't keep him from it." She began another nosedive. Tears welled. "This time it was cousin Son Jayroe's Buick Skylark that Son paid umpteen-thousand dollars for. Son loved that car better than his bride Tawny Louise. Lou was best man at their wedding, looked like a movie star in his tuxedo. I was maid-of-honor in a Virginia Mayo pink formal, my hair piled up, glitter dust sprinkled all through. Lou said I was the most ravishing piece of anything he'd ever seen. We went to Jimbo's Jumbo Room for the reception, then me and Lou drove the bride and groom to the airport in Son's Skylark. Lord, how Lou loved driving that car, sitting in his fancy tuxedo, foot flat on the gas. When we hit El Paso, Lou drove out to the airport and me and Son and Tawny Louise stepped outta that convertible like kings and queens. They was fly'n to Baton Rouge for their honeymoon and had three big suitcases stuffed in the trunk. Before Son could find someone to haul 'em out, Lou took off to park. I reckon New York City was about the nearest slot. Son went berserk, dashed all over Texas with a gun looking for Lou, but none of us ever saw him or that tuxedo or the Skylark again. 'Cept me, cause I got that postcard and jumped the Grey-dawg to come see him. Only he wasn't wearing the tux and instead of the Skylark he was driving this junky Hudson and you was married to him."

Son Jayroe? Tawny Louise? Joke names. Slapstick characters. Who but the utterly absurd held wedding receptions in places like Jimbo's Jumbo Room or suffered the indignity of the best man stealing the groom's car? Sideshow performers like Son and Tawny Louise, that's who. And here was Miss Laura Dark

Eyes, living witness to the debacle. Marta knew, of course, these characters were absolutely real, their lives testaments to the lunacy of truth. Now she was among them, maybe always had been—fleeing Louisville in hope of escaping them—an auditor and, by implication, a participant, wed in fact to one of the principal perpetrators. She grasped the wheel as if to keep from swerving off the road. Good God, she thought, here I sit laughing at this mixed-up little nobody while I sink deeper into a jam-up so bad it would take Harry Houdini to get me out.

Sensing Marta's despair, Dark Eyes screwed up her strawberry mouth and cried harder than ever.

"If you want," Marta said, "I'll climb in back and sit with you."

"You don't wanna." She thrashed about the back seat, dark hair tossing into her ashen face. "You don't wanna touch me. You think you're better'n me. You don't care if I croak, just so you can go on without me " Suddenly, jerking the straps of her chemise from her shoulders as if to bare her scars, she yanked the garment to her waist. Bones. Bone white flesh. This is it, Marta thought, she's coming right out of her skin. Half naked, the girl tumbled through the door into the road.

"Laura!" Marta scrambled from the car but the girl was up and running. "Laura, for God's sake!"

It was dusk. Lights of distant farms glowed yellow in the empty landscape. After thirty yards Marta ran down the girl, spun her around. Spindly arms circled her, the stricken face pressed wetly at her neck. "Don't leave me," Dark Eyes cried. "Please, don't leave me." Looping an arm around her waist, Marta walked Dark Eyes back to the car. Across the road a black-and-white trooper's car cruised past, made a U-turn, eased up beside them.

"You two females having trouble?"

Backed against the Hudson, Marta and Dark Eyes looked into a beefsteak face smirking beneath the slant of a trooper's hat.

Marta maneuvered the girl's chemise over her chest but the cop already had an eyeful.

"Something wrong with the car," Marta stammered. "Husband's in town fetching a mechanic."

"Any excuse your friend here's running around in public with nothing but her, ah, night clothes." The trooper's gaze slid down Dark Eye's body.

Marta pulled the trembling girl against her. "You okay?"

Dark Eyes tried to smile. "Okay," she said, hands shielding her body.

The trooper's eyes licked up. Though the girl had sold herself on St. Louis street corners, she was pricing herself out of this market and he knew it.

"Don't know where you two come from," he said, hooking thumbs into a bullet-studded belt, "but in this state it's a crime to expose yourself indecently in public."

"It ain't like I was exactly naked."

He stepped nearer, looped a finger under the strap of her chemise, pulled it away from her breasts and made a leisurely examination. "I could run you in, you know. Wouldn't be the first time from the looks of you." He knew a hooker when he saw one, knew how to treat her. Releasing the strap he stepped back. "You know what you get for soliciting in this state? Six months, that's what. Courtesy of the governor."

"Gimme a break. I ain't solicited nothin' from nobody."

"Don't kid me, I heard you saying as how you'd show me a good time on the backseat for a dollar. Besides, a girl out in public with as little on as you can't be doing nothing but soliciting."

"It's fever," Marta blurted, drawing Dark Eyes closer, cradling her face against her shoulder. "My sister's got the fever."

The trooper stepped back. "Mean she's sick?"

"Burning up. Can't wear a stitch more or she'd explode."

"What's she got?"

"Diphtheria, looks like. Or smallpox. Hard to tell at the contagious stage." She stated this flatly, a chuckleheaded ploy remembered from some otherwise forgotten movie. Jerking off his hat that exposed a Nazi crewcut, the trooper nodded gravely, believing every word.

"Get her in the car and out of sight. I'll check the motor. You better get to a doctor in town."

It was dirt in the fuel line, a little daub of goop no bigger than a match head that the trooper held in his palm.

When she finally found Lou drinking gin rickeys in the bar of the Hotel Peru and told him, he shrugged. "It'd take a damn cop to find a little bitty piece of shit like that." Prying him from his drink and the small-town boozers listening to his lies, she drove to a motor court on the outskirts of town. Dark Eyes crouched in the car while Lou and Marta carried their bags into an icy one-room cabin, then smuggled Dark Eyes inside. She went straight to the only chair, a dusty, overstuffed maroon relic and curled up.

"I spotted a Chinese place uptown," Lou said, cocking the brim of his fedora. "I'll get us some takeout and beer. You two need cheering up."

Marta unpacked her imitation leopard coat and spread it over the girl. "You want to sleep in the bed, go ahead. I'd as soon sleep in the chair."

Dark Eyes rubbed the tatty, spotted cloth as if caressing a living animal. "What about him?" she asked.

"Lou? I don't figure he can do much he hasn't done before —to you and everyone else from here to Wink and back."

"I'm sorry for what I said, about him being a stud horse and all. When I found out you was married to him I figured I'd give as good as I got. I didn't mean no harm."

Marta sat on the bed and slipped off her shoes. "I'll survive."

"You think he would'a come back for us? I mean, with a

mechanic and everything? You think he would'a really showed?"

"In his own good time. He sent you that postcard, didn't he? When the moment comes you want to shake him, Lou Sinclair will be a hard man to lose."

"You thinkin' of that?"

"Thinking of it, yeah. I reckon most brides do. It's a basic part of marriage. Did you ever see one of those air shows they put on at county fairs? One of those high flying acts where a woman in goggles and overalls climbs from the cockpit while the pilot puts the plane through loop-the-loops and snap rolls? She works her way out between the struts and guy wires to the end of the wing, then waves to the crowd below. You know the trick that keeps her from falling? She never lets go with one hand until she's got a firm grip on something solid with the other.

"I didn't think about that when I got on the Greyhound down in Louisville and rode up to New York. There wasn't anything between me and the ground but $200 and blind luck. Never again. I make any more big moves, I'll be a real wing walker. And if I have to turn loose before I should, I'll be sure there's something soft to land on."

"If you turn loose of Lou, just point him in my direction. Lord, what that man does to me ain't fit for decent folks to think about."

"So you said."

"Sorry." Dark Eyes quietly stroked the leopard coat. Her eyes met Marta's. "I'm always puttin' my foot in my mouth. I never was a cool number like you. The way you handled that cop this afternoon was really somethin'. I met plenty like him before —they'll screw you over, bust you up, then in you go for resisting arrest. If it wasn't for you, I'd be coolin' it in the county tank. You're one levelheaded lady."

Marta edged into the massive, stone-cold bed, resolved she'd find a way to help Dark Eyes. She couldn't drift another minute. Destruction lay around the corner: cigarette dangling, hat tugged low, gorilla body wrapped in a ratty trench coat. Played out by the long day, Marta fought to clear her mind, find the first step.

Lou slid in beside her.

"You awake?"

She didn't answer.

"Come on, catfish, give us a sign."

Before she opened her eyes and faced the raw spring morning, she knew Dark Eyes and the leopard coat were gone. She sat up quickly and looked into the empty chair. Lou stood above the bed, holding two paper cups of coffee.

"Okay," Marta asked, "where is she?"

Lou offered coffee. "With cream an' sugah fo'ah my swee' lady."

"Cut the darky talk. What have you done with that girl?"

"Little Miss Laura?"

"That poor hooker you've been living off of for God knows how long."

"Darlin', you don't know I've lived off anybody, except maybe you. You've helped me a lot and I won't forget it. You're paying into a sure-fire organization and when things get right with me, you'll collect in spades. Now drink your coffee before it gets cold."

Marta dragged a blanket across her shoulders and drank her coffee. "What about my coat?"

Lou slouched in the chair. "I couldn't haul her around any longer with hardly nothin' on, now could I? We get to a place that's got decent stores, I'll get you a real one—one made outta honest-to-God cat. One won't smell like it died every time it rains. Can't deny that po' girl use of your coat when you got a man promises to buy you a new cat coat first chance. Darlin', you got a bigger heart than that."

Did she? She'd gone to bed determined she'd see the girl through. No longer possible, she felt a sweeping sense of relief.

"We could have bought her a bus ticket," she said. "We could have driven her to the station and seen her on her way. She could have gone back to Wink and taken up whatever she did before she left." Knowing she'd lost, it was easy to put up a fight. "We could have taken her with us. Maybe she could drive. We might have traded off."

"We might have traded off, all right," Lou said, licking a finger and smoothing the pale crescents of his eyebrows. "Only I misdoubt it'd been driving."

"Couldn't let that go, could you?" She shook her head. "You've got a mind like a sewer, Lou. A goddamn cesspool."

He smiled, cocking his hands behind his head. "Least I wasn't so mean as to put her on the Greydawg and send her back to Wink, where she'd spend the rest of her life in the gutter or jail. And I didn't see much future in draggin' her around with us. With you and me so tight, she'd bound to feel left out."

"What was your alternative? Send her to the college of her choice in my leopard coat?"

"She's had all the education she needs. Ready to turn full-time pro. I just helped her find work. I know folks here and over in Cicero that will see she gets a bed, three squares and somethin' to keep her busy." Lou moved toward Marta, spread his fingers around her neck, easing her face against his thigh. "Lou's seen the little girl through."

She couldn't move, her face frozen to his trousers, even though what he'd done was worse than she'd imagined. By not helping the girl herself, not giving her the coat and putting her on the bus, she was as much to blame.

"What you've done . . . ." She searched for the right phrase. "Is . . . is to . . . ." What she came up with sounded old-fashioned, a tag her mother would have used watching a soldier-boy escort a flashy blond into the lobby of Brown's Hotel. "You've sold her into white slavery!"

Lou doubled over, laughing.

"It isn't goddamn funny. It's exactly what you've done. You've taken money. The kid hasn't a chance. She'll be dead at thirty and you'll be to blame."

Lou's eyes rolled. "Me? A good old boy like me?" He drew her against him. "Marta, darlin', would Lou do something like that? Would he sell a flower of Southern womanhood like our little Laura fo'ah thutty pieces of sil-vah? Am I Judas Iscariot? If that's what you think, darlin', you got me all wrong—but you sure enough got me!"

He pulled her near, a hand turning her face. His flat, water-colored eyes shone with amusement.

"Got me. Hear?"

And she did.

Reno

She was right—Lou had sold the girl for thirty pieces of silver and, one bleak and freezing afternoon, did his best to pawn Marta off in exchange for a gambling debt.

They finally reached Reno, stayed at the El Encanto, a cluster of pastel boxes awash in a pool of neon out North Virginia Street. Their neighbors were Shastans, Washos, Karoks, Klamaths— abandoned people living along the edges of muddy roads in abandoned cars, camping trailers, shacks built of rusty Coca-Cola signs and shot-up sheets of corrugated tin. Riding home from her bookkeeping job at Harrah's with Pammy Lea Barker, a bleached-blond blackjack dealer who lived next door, Marta stared at the vacant, moonlike faces of children pressed to the windows of inadvertent dwellings and felt neither sorrow nor compassion—but a rising panic as if she too were sealed away in tombs of the living, stripped of identity, without a future. Something must happen, she told herself. Something's got to change.

The something arrived in the form of Carl Drexler, a gangling, rawboned ex-Marine who ran a roadside bordello out Route 80. There, where cinder-block buildings squatted in high-desert sage far from Reno's neon, Lou did his gambling and whoring. Whether he went into debt on Drexler's poker tables or his girls, Marta never knew. It didn't matter, Drexler told her, stretched comfortably in black Stetson and stained undershorts across Marta's double bed. The important thing was that he held a fistful of Lou's IOUs. Ways had been devised for their redemption.

She stood in the open doorway, the frozen landscape a shabby tent behind her. Drexler studied her the way a man studies a rabbit trapped in the headlights of his speeding car. A great clot of butter-colored phlegm covered one eye. Through this eye he viewed the world.

"Shut the door and get outta your clothes," he ordered, reaching into his shorts and hefting what was there. "I come to sample the merchandise."

Numb with incomprehension she stared at the hairless torso, the pale collection of graceless limbs, the awful eye.

Drexler's face softened, mistaking her look for one of interest. His lips peeled back in an appalling grin.

The grin did it, triggered the click in Marta's brain, an actual click that told her the moment had come when she would take control of her life.

Drexler's eye still on her, she stepped back and slammed the door. In Pammy Lea's apartment she told the girl to drive her downtown.

"We just come from there. Besides, I got a date in a hour. I gotta fix up."

"Forget the date. This is important. I've got a bus to catch."

"I didn't know. Where you going?"

"Carson City—but it's not where, it's what I'll do when I get there."

"Well, what? What's the darn rush?"

"Because I'm getting a D-I-V-O-R-C-E. Now shake a leg before it's too late."

The last Marta saw of the ex-Marine he was hopping from foot to foot on the frozen parking lot, trying to pull on his boots as Pammy's mud-spattered Cadillac churned out of the drive and sped toward town.

San Francisco to Santa Barbara

She was right on another score: Lou was hard to shake. Even after she arrived in San Francisco and found a job in an accountant's office in the Matson Building, she sometimes found him on Market Street when she came down from work.

"Marta, darlin', how are you? You look ravishing. How'd you like to step out with an old rascal like me? We could have a drink before you run off to dinner with one of your high-toned beaus."

"Sorry, Lou, not tonight. Having cocktails on Nob Hill — invitees only. Next time, call and you can take me to dinner."

Finally he came to Marta's Presidio Heights apartment and escorted her to a small, expensive French place on the fringe of North Beach. Afterward, they drank Irish coffees at the Buena Vista. She eyed him over her glass, his pale hair clipped and clean, his skin a healthy pink.

"Something good has happened to you," she said.

"Reckon I found my niche."

"I'd say you've moved into a new realm."

"Think we both have." He raised his glass. "To us, jus' friends."

"Jus' friends," she murmured, thoughts buzzing with Irish whisky. Jus' friends? Should she be jus' a friend and forgive?

For a while they met once a week for drinks and dinner, then once or twice a month. Finally a year slipped past before she lifted the receiver to hear, "Marta, darlin', it's me."

After she married Josh and moved to Santa Barbara, Lou occasionally appeared, usually at Birnam Wood or Talk of the Town, always a different willowy, vacant-eyed creature in *haute couture* swaying on his arm. "Pub-lick ree-lations," he answered whenever someone asked his business, as if this explained the woman, his manner, the carefully manicured drawl and a suggestion of makeup coloring his face.

The makeup caught her eye when she saw Lou after an interval of years. She and Josh had ridden to the Coral Casino in their Jag saloon. There was a dinner-dance for charity: orphans, drug addicts or crippled children, if anyone cared. Followed by a floor show: bankers in blackface, horsey young society matrons flashing ruffled panties in a cancan. Big, bland Josh, cetaceous in a rumpled tux, beelined for the bar and a lineup of double martinis. Marta looked for someone she knew. There was Princess Cavadini holding court with her gay entourage near the inevitable potted palm and, nearby, the aging Doris Fox admiring her silver wig in a mirror. Through a glazed arch she watched Josh lift an iced glass against a face flushed by early cocktails. Like the Central High prom, she thought, wandering beneath balloons and paper streamers. Boys drinking while the girls gossip. The same drab decorations and dull music. Hopes a little tattered now, but hopes all the same: dreams of possibility and romance, dreams going fast. Shaking the thought, she wondered where to present her smile, the negotiable coin of "Hello."

He stood across the room. She couldn't believe it, not until he grinned.

"Marta, darlin', is it really you?"

He held her hands as they studied one another. Suddenly she was twenty again, clasped in his supple arms, swaying across the vast floor at Roseland. He hadn't aged. The cosmetics were an affectation. Not a line touched his face, his body trim as ever in an impeccable tuxedo. Of course he escorted the most eligible divorcee in a neighborhood noted for eligible divorcees. He pointed her out across the dance floor. Elegant and beautiful, at ease in her abandonment. Marta was charmed.

"She's stunning," she said. "You're very lucky."

"And you?"

"All right. Life goes on. I've no real complaints."

"You're looking older."

"Older?"

"You should take better care of yourself." He spoke with the authority of one who's spent a large part of his life in steam rooms. Lifting her hands, he turned them over. For a moment she thought he would kiss them like an Italian count. "Liver spots," he said. "Do yourself a favor, see a dermatologist. I can send you to an excellent man in Beverly Hills. He works wonders. While you're at it, wouldn't hurt to have a tuck or two taken—" A manicured finger, the nail polished and bright as ice, traced her mouth, touched the corner of her eye. "—here and here. Turn you into a new woman. Jazz you up a little, Marta darlin'."

He walked away, narrow hips swaying like a tango dancer's as he passed among the tables. He leaned forward to kiss his divorcee on the curve of her throat.

Straightening, Marta smoothed her dress, touched her hair, fingered a curl at her temple. She was halfway to the ladies' room before she screamed.

WANAMAKER

Brenda MacMasters was into her warmup. The men's race, the Wanamaker Mile, finished—a near record performance from Eamonn Coghlan and Thomas Wessinghage. Some of the spectators headed up the aisles. They'd hoped for a Coe-Ovett duel but the organizers hadn't put the package together. The world's two best milers had stayed in England. In the duel department the fans had to settle for Brenda and me.

Brenda worked an easy jog along the backstretch as I moved out at a slightly faster pace. Before I reached her she stepped off the track to talk with someone. When I sailed past, she called, "Hi, Sherry!" I waved and went on.

We didn't come face to face until we'd pulled off our sweats and stepped toward the starting line. Brenda was small and thin, with fine bones and ginger hair neatly coiled in braids on the sides of her head. She had pale green eyes, beautiful, almost translucent skin, and a quiet smile so elusive you were never certain it was there. At first sight she seemed ghostlike. Later, when you got to know her, she was warm and easygoing. She never griped or complained; nothing showed of the brute pain she'd known: pulled muscles, torn ligaments, tendinitis, compartment syndrome, hours on operating tables and weeks of recuperation. Nor was there a sign of the will, the heart, strength, the pure ambition and killer instinct that drove her.

"Hi. How you doing?"

"Okay. You?"

"Fine. Good luck."

"Thanks. You too."

We shook hands up and down the line—six of us. The TAC 800-meter champ Maxine Newman was in lane one. She'd do the pace-setting. Brenda in lane two. I came next, then Grace Johnson, Debbie Schafer and a newcomer, Ann Hatcher.

When the starter called us to the line, all the plans, calculations, months of training compressed into an instant. I knew I wasn't ready. Across the track in the first row of seats, Mom and my brother Orrin cheered and waved while Daddy stood to the side, arms folded, nodding encouragement. T.S., my trainer, was somewhere in the infield crowd, clock in hand. I wanted to yell, you're wasting your time. I haven't a chance in hell.

When the starter called us to our marks I glanced at Brenda, who looked at me. Neither of us spoke. Reaching toward me, she brushed my shoulder with the tips of her fingers. Only that. A gesture so brief not one of the twenty thousand spectators probably noticed or, if they did, understood.

But we did. We knew that running up so near the edge takes its toll. You get hurt, try to figure out why you do this. Not finding an answer, you simply pick yourself up and try again. Everyone expects it. You expect it. The alternative is a slow irreversible winding down. To beat it, you've got to beat yourself.

Sharing that knowledge eased the doubt. Leaning forward, I wanted to hug Brenda, tell her thanks. I knew what Brenda wanted and would do it. This was no kid's footrace down a wind-washed beach, but the real thing, a run toward the farthest edge. Brenda was attacking her own national record, trying to force herself beyond a barrier of her creation. Maxine would pace her. I would push. That was what Brenda wanted. Maybe, just maybe, if I pushed hard and fast enough, I could make a final rush for the record itself.

Brenda knew that.

Knowing it created the possibility.

In an instant I went from hope to despair to hope again. The starter's arm rose, then held motionless, the hot light from the arc lamps catching the crimson folds of his false satin sleeve, the soft sheen of the snub-nosed pistol in his pink fist. My eyes shifted from the gun to the empty track—the blank space I somehow had to fill. I tensed toward it, weight distributed so that bone and muscle strained forward. I took a deep breath. The count went to three. The gun fired.

Maxine went out first, just as planned, smooth raven arms pumping, the bright beads strung on her corn-rowed hair bobbing in counterpoint to the rhythm of her running. Brenda came next. I followed, tight on her shoulder. We broke from the chute and leaned into the first turn, stride for stride in perfect order, locked like cars on a short fast freight. We held on through the turn. Maxine ate up the track with that mean half-mile pace that made her famous, pulling Brenda and me as if she'd created a vacuum in her wake. Already, the fear, pain and despair had vanished, replaced by euphoria. I was on top of things when we sailed out of the first turn and into the backstretch. With an extra effort I pulled up beside Brenda, matched her pace for a moment, then slipped ahead to find myself on Maxine's heels. Score one for Sherry. The crowd began a muffled roar as the three of us charged furiously down the back straight toward the turn.

Ten-and-a-quarter laps. 146.341 meters per lap. 1500

meters. A kilometer and a half. Down only 120 meters and already I had come up with a surprise, had the speed to stay with Maxine, the guts to make a move in the opening lap and pass Brenda. With the race only eighteen or nineteen seconds old, Brenda was forced to make calculations, develop new tactics. Calculations take energy; energy steals time. And I breezed along, sucked up on Maxine's heels, with no place to go but home.

Breaking out of the turn and into the straight, you could hear Mom and Orrin hollering, beating time with their hands, voices an octave higher than the drone of the packed house. Daddy's voice, familiar, came to me through the megaphone of his cupped hands.

"Stay with it, Sherry. Stay with the pace. Don't give an inch!"

Up the straight and into the turn and out again, remembering the things T.S. had taught me: lean in early, straighten up late, run tall, don't chop. I remembered his warnings, too: chop and break and you'll put too big a load on your sockets and joints. Watch for trouble in your hips, knees and ankles. Watch for pain. It tells you something. But there was no pain. I felt like spring water flowing down a mountain cut. Flying the back straight for the second time I spotted T.S. in the infield and wanted to tell him: Yes, it's come together. It's all come together now. There was no need. He knew. Knew by the way I glided by on Maxine's trail and swept again into the bottom turn.

We held it steady, steady and straight. I'd never run so smoothly, so effortlessly. Breaking out of the turn, we started down the stretch and into the third lap. This was the important one —the big third. When we began our lean into the second turn, we'd hit the first quarter-mile. An official would call our time. Was the pace fast enough? Was a try for the record really on? This early in the race it was up to Maxine. Perfectly tuned to her job, she pulled me with her, Brenda a step behind. The others straggled, or so I imagined. I concentrated only on Maxine's swaying shoulders, the blue and yellow beads bobbing at the nape of her neck.

We sailed the backstretch at the same solid pace, streaked by faces lining the infield. Ahead, an official in an outside lane held a stopwatch before narrowed eyes. His voice barked as we swept past:

"Sixty-point three, sixty-point four, sixty-point five."

By the time we hit mid-curve, the public address system crackled the news: "Unofficially, at the quarter, sixty-point-three." A note of disbelief sounded in the announcer's voice. A second later he boomed: "Officially, sixty-point-one! Not even the men in the Wanamaker Mile ran the first quarter that fast!"

We were on our way, the record a real possibility, running three-tenths of a second ahead of Brenda's first-quarter split when she cracked the record two years before. The drone of the crowd turned into a throbbing roar. We were on. This was it—the big one. I started to panic.

Had Maxine taken us out too fast? Could I hold the pace? The quickest first quarter split I'd ever run was sixty-one flat, and that had proved too demanding. I was left flatfooted when the leaders began their kick. Now I waited for the pain, waited for my starved muscles to scream for oxygen. I was tired. I'd ruined a year's training in a single day. The pain would begin soon—pulled tendons, hairline fractures spider-webbing my anklebones.

Going into the second quarter Maxine eased the pace. The pain, if it were coming, wouldn't come yet. Brenda wouldn't make her move, not as long as Maxine was out there. Her bid would come later, her fantastic last-lap kick, when there was only Sherry left to challenge. For the next sixty seconds I could relax a little, settle into the number-two slot and coast toward the half-mile.

Round and round the banked-board track, pounding down

straightaways, angling through turns. The crowd chanted and clapped, feet stamping in unison with the strained, hypnotic "Go! Go! Go!"

Everyone wants to be a part of something special. You can't blame them. When a politician shakes your hand, then wins big, you're part of it, part of a front-running team. Cheering someone on to a touchdown or record-cracking leap puts an extra point on your emotional scoreboard. Now they were after Maxine, Brenda and me to give that touch of excitement to the end of their evening.

"Go! Go! Go!"

But they couldn't rush Maxine. She was too experienced. Holding a steady pace, she brought us into lap five. Halfway through we would hit the half-mile, our second split, and be on our own. And then? It was up to me to display the solid nerves and world-class maturity I wasn't sure I had. We'd see. Everyone was so sure I had it in me: Daddy and T.S., Orrin and Mom; no one blinked when they spoke of my being on top. The only way I could prove it was to do it. It had seemed so right and easy to step ahead of Brenda, but the moment might come when I would have to pay my dues.

We broke from the turn and halfway down the back straight the face was there again: "Two-oh-four-four, two-oh-four-five, two-oh-four-six."

We'd slacked off the first quarter pace but were still on schedule. Everything was possible if I kept the power going and nerves under control. But this was the moment I dreaded. A few strides beyond the timer, Maxine spurted ahead and at the top of the turn, her job done, stepped off the track. Suddenly, leaning through the curve and pounding into the straight, I found myself in front.

Faced with leading, my fear vanished. The next quarter-mile rippled past in a dream of gold medals and the flame of an

Olympic torch, running in front while twenty thousand fans looked on, cheering. Yet knowing Brenda was right on my shoulder, matching me stride for stride, ready, whenever she gave the command, to shift gears and make her challenge. But not yet. As long as I felt the pressure and held the pace, Brenda would stay put.

The thirteen-twenty fell away in three-ten flat, the announcement nearly drowned by the crowd's roaring. This final clocking wasn't really important. We were already committed. There was no turning back since the gun fired and we broke for position. Now, with 300 meters, a couple of steps more than two laps to go, the price of that commitment had to be paid.

Incredibly, there was no pain. I knew then it wouldn't come. My legs spun solidly over the banked boards, the spring still in them. Only now I felt the beginning of strain, the sense of fatigue when you've pushed yourself as near the edge as possible. And with it, feeling excitement, joy, anticipation, apprehension, because you know that in the next few seconds you'll have to find a way to go into territory you've never traveled.

Starting into the next-to-last lap, I picked up the pace. It wasn't the start of my kick, nothing so bold as that, just edging up the throttle that half notch Maxine had backed off after the first quarter. An explosion of approval echoed through the Garden. The clapping and foot stomping lost cadence and became a general thunderous roar. I tried to shake the noise, keep my head clear. Steady. Don't blow it now. Steady as she goes.

Coming out of the turn, Brenda was still a half step back of my right shoulder. Make your move, I thought. I'm ready. But she held, an unshakable shadow, matching my stride.

Halfway down the backstretch I spotted T.S. waving his arms and hollering something I couldn't hear. When I came alongside, he ran with me for a few steps, pushing past officials and security police, shouting encouragement until I lost him and leaned into the turn, sensing something behind me, a new pressure building at my back.

Don't look. Run your race and let the others take care of themselves. A quick glance back can prove the beginning of the end. It had before. But the pressure was there. Someone besides Brenda pushing. I waited until we passed the top of the turn and moved into the straight before I gave in, turning my head abruptly to the left. In that instant I saw Debbie Ann Schaefer, her blond face set with determination, only a step behind and forcing the pace. Then Brenda shifted into overdrive, sprinted past me on the right, letting loose the power of her tremendous kick.

My own kick triggered spontaneously and we slammed out of the turn. The bell sounded for the final lap. The three of us were less than a step apart.

Who knows what makes you go when there's nothing left. Guts, competitiveness, call it what you want. You just hold yourself together and put one foot down in front of the other.

But the damage was done. The pace too fast. I'd forced myself to the edge and didn't like what I saw on the other side. Not poor training or some fault of nerves, but the dispiriting power of another doing what you do, only doing it better. Watching Brenda edge away I knew immediately that all the training in the world wouldn't make me number one. Brenda was too powerful.

Still, I held on. You don't quit because you're behind. That's one of the rules. My muscles uncoiled with a fluidity that amazed me, my blood pumping energy like fire. I would never run this well again. Everything aligned, everything worked to perfection. Everything, of course, except Brenda.

And now there was Debbie Ann moving up on my right, hanging at my elbow, ready to make her bid. As we broke from the next-to-last turn, she moved nearer. My only hope was to hold her on the outside, force her to take the extra steps that running the outside means. Leaning into the turn she came on. Then, from somewhere behind, breaking through the roar, a single, familiar voice cut down the track. Not Daddy's or T.S.'s, but my brother Orrin's, loud and childish, almost worshipful, filled with wild optimism: "GO FOR IT, SHERRY! GO FOR IT!"

It was as silly and unreal as a scene from *Andy Hardy* or *Happy Days*. Orrin's words got through and I felt myself slip into a new gear. Felt Debbie Ann start to fade. Through the turn I gained a step on Brenda, but hitting the top of the backstretch her stride lengthened and I watched her slide away.

Debbie Ann challenged again, chasing me through the final curve, breaking up beside me as we sprinted into the home stretch. She meant business, jostling me with an elbow as she moved a step ahead. I kept my momentum and, back on pace, fought toward the finish. Beyond thinking, beyond anything except letting my body do what it was trained to do—run free and hard into the emptiness. Because Brenda was gone now, through the tape and into the infield as Debbie and I went stride-for-stride through the last ten meters. In the final second, I lunged ahead.

Pandemonium, dizzying waves of exhaustion. Daddy charged toward me, grinning bravely. "You broke four minutes. You're sub-four, Pumpkin. Sub-*four*!" There was only nerve-shattering light as I faded into Daddy's arms, knowing I'd never do this again.

CHEVY IN THE FAST LANE

Gaining the final rise, the car begins its descent before Vince realizes it. The coolness of the fog-bound coast behind, he feels the first sweltering gusts lift from the furnace of the valley floor. Two weeks, he thinks, bearing down on the accelerator, and I've already forgotten what it is. Christ, you've got to be nuts to go down there. Positively insane.

Even the bland and incorporeal music seeping from the radio changes as the Chevy noses into downward curves. The cool night music of the urban coast, resonant with clusters of strings and horns, pianos gliding over endless soft cadenzas, the occasional icy blare of an alto sax, gives way to static, then nothing before the sudden charged and plaintive pessimism of country takes over with quavering voices and weeping steel guitars: "Lovesick Blues," "Is Anybody Going North to Cincinnati," "I'm Moving On."

Abruptly, he shuts the music off. Now only the steady hum of tires on hot pavement. A sound he likes, probably more than any other. This and the sound of a train, a freight chuffing ponderously across a long night. And the low, comforting wink of the car's dash lights, the blaze of headlights scanning black lanes ahead. The highway is divided into three lanes either way. Those heading west are a mile to his left across a down-slanting moonscape of jumbled stone. Easing the wheel, he steers through a long, banked curve, then across an open span bridging a rock-walled arroyo that falls away deep and unseen on either side. A semi-trailer, geared low against the grade, labors downward at midspan. The Chevy's high beams dip; the lights blink off and instantly on again. The trucker blinks his own, rows of red and amber bulbs flashing as the Chevy rocks into the outside lane and hurtles past. Again, the ritual of lights. An instant of communication between two speeding drivers before the Chevy rushes alone toward the span's down-curving end, the stony ridges beyond.

Vince loves this speed, this wide, fast road curving across the night. His hands steady the wheel, foot to the floor. He's satisfied, fulfilled, in control of things. Someday he'll make a really big trip. Nonstop: L.A. to Vegas, Vegas to Salt Lake, then Route 80 right up the middle of the country, splitting it like the overripe melon it is—Salt Lake, Cheyenne, Omaha, Chicago, South Bend, Toledo, and on through Ohio and up the Pennsylvania Turnpike into New York. New York. The Big Apple. He smiles thinking of it, but wonders what he'll do once he got there. Drink a few beers, get laid, sleep six hours, then head straight back. He's never been east of Tulsa and sees no sense in going that far, except for this, this driving, the road running on, headlights tracking down bleak slopes of barren mountains.

They're different now, he thinks, these roads, freeways, cutting six lanes over wild country. He remembers this stretch just a few years ago when it took forever to cover a hundred miles on two lanes of patched asphalt. There were towns along the way— tiny, godforsaken places, but towns all the same. Places where people lived and puttered at odd jobs and went half-insane from idleness and isolation: Descanso, Wisteria, Jacumba, Plaster City, Dixieland, Coyote Wells. Places where you gassed up and ate chili and a slice of homemade pie, then browsed through a roadside stand selling dates and honey and pale yellow grapefruit by the crate. And there was always a beer joint where you could live on draft beer and pigs's knuckles and stay for days.

He wonders if they still exist, strung along roads no one uses anymore. Except maybe the townspeople, backtracking from one crossroads to another, looking for amusement and trouble and a few dollars to add to welfare payments and social security checks. He misses these stops, the isolated faces of people used to strangers passing through. He even misses that patched, twisting road, knowing that when you finally got to where you were going, you would step from the car, stretch, and say: "Well, goddamn, I made it!"

Now it's like flying, driving these freeways with all the bends and towns taken out, the scenery going by so fast you can't tell the difference between a signpost and a wrecked car somebody's run off an embankment. But there are compensations, he thinks, guiding the car through a sweeping curve and on across a brush-covered plateau. He relishes the rush forward, the feeling of omnipotence that comes from controlling the vast length of empty highway.

He slows at the top of Mountain Springs Pass, turns onto an off-ramp and follows an access road into a sprawling, brightly lit service area. The gas station, its blue-tiled roof set atop glass-and-concrete walls, stands amid a vastness of asphalt. Open 24 Hours! Nearby, a coffee shop blazes under the same merciless lights.

The car parked at the pumps, Vince leans against a Coke machine, watching a black youth in coveralls fill the Chevy's tank. The young man cleans the windshield, then steps under the lights, wiping his hands on an oily rag. Vince eyes his smooth approach, the way he moves with the cool grace of a golf pro crossing a green on television. Deftness in others irritates him, as if his bigness, his own heavy motion, is being mocked. When the black, unsmiling face draws near Vince flashes a credit card, then withdraws it.

"Oil and water okay?" he asks, staring into expressionless eyes.

The young man doesn't flinch. "Sure. Fine. Everything's okay."

Vince shrugs, shaking his head. He's five inches taller, a hundred pounds heavier than the black. "You didn't check them."

"How you mean?"

"What I said. You didn't check them. You don't know if that car's got any damn oil in it or not."

The attendant shrugs. "Suit yourself." No apology in his quiet voice. Executing a slow spin, he glides smoothly back toward the car.

"And check the tires," Vince shouts after him. "And have a look at the battery, while you're at it."

With the Chevy's hood lifted and the black's back bent over a fender, Vince slides into the office. He makes no pretense of looking at road maps, fan belts, shelves stacked with car wax and rust preventative, but heads straight to a large metal desk. Beneath the cracked glass covering it, among yellowed business cards, tax tables and pages torn from parts catalogs, he finds a recent print-out of lost and stolen credit cards. He scans it twice. The card in the name of Burt Wallace, cupped in Vince's palm, is not among them.

Two weeks and the good luck holds, he thinks, strolling back to the car. It's what that idiot Burt Wallace, whoever he is, deserves, marrying a hot little redhead who's too dumb and scared to tell her old man the card was lifted from her purse by a guy she's been balling in a Del Mar motel. The Del Mar trip was good for a double score. With a little luck, such things could go on forever. But he can't always take these chances. In a few days he'll have to destroy the card. For now, he'll enjoy it. He smiles, passing it into the attendant's hand.

In the coffee shop, Vince eats a tasteless burger, a slice of pie, drinks a greasy cup of warm coffee. Down the counter, the waitress, a rubber-tipped pencil shoved into the intricacies of her bleached hair, snaps gum and chats with the only other customer, a young man in a Stetson, a toothpick dangling from his lip. A medley of famous movie themes oozes over hidden speakers. As he chokes down the stale food, Vince notices the cook's weary eyes staring from the kitchen.

Outside, the euphoria he felt in the service station vanishes. Hands shoved deep into pockets, he walks to the car, head bowed, kicking stones, unaware of the boy in the Stetson just steps behind.

In the underlighting from the dash the boy's face is not so young. Lines edge tired eyes; a reddish stubble shadows sunken cheeks. With a sucking sound he works the toothpick over his lips, scowling.

"How far you say you'd take me?"

"Didn't."

"Oh."

"Don't worry I'll get you down the road a way."

They ride on in silence. Behind, a moon hangs in a star-bright sky. The mazy jumble of stony, brush-covered hills, the distant valley floor glow in ghostly illumination. The Chevy races across the top of moonlit ridges, then drops between sheer granite walls of a descending gorge.

"I don't usually pick anybody up."

Vince waits. There's no response. Turning, he sees the lean

face, surly and withdrawn.

"The way I travel, I can't take chances." Vince's fingers drum the wheel. "You drive as much as I do, the odds build up against you. Know what I mean? Too many creeps on the road these days. Too many people begging for handouts. More and more people getting like that: welfare cases, guys jamming arms into machinery so they can collect compensation, Mexican field hands starting up rebel unions, kids hitting you for change. You read about it every day. People think the world owes them a living. And the hitchhikers! Mostly healthy guys who should be earning a living. There they are, standing all over the roads, until there are hardly enough cars to haul them around. And now there're these sexy young girls asking for lifts, then hollering 'rape' so you have to pay them off before they call a cop. You know what I'd do if a girl tried that?"

Vince glances at the rider. No response. A waxen profile, toothpick dangling from lifeless lips.

"I'd kill her," Vince says flatly. "And that goes for any creep with a knife or gun. Anybody fucks with me, I'll rip them apart. You've got to handle yourself like that. You can't let people shit on you. Know what I mean?"

"Look, you didn't have to give me a ride." The voice high-pitched, strained, words choked out. "You could have said no. You could have left me standing back there."

"That's all right. Don't take it personal. I was only talking. Sometimes when you're driving, you like to have somebody to talk to, someone to keep you awake.

"Well, anytime you want, you can just let me off. When we come to the next service area, just pull over and I'll get out."

"That's okay. Don't let it worry you. I'll get you down the road."

The car speeds downward. Holding the speedometer at a steady ninety, Vince watches the broken center line flash past. He thinks of Angel Ortega, picturing him in dusty white, hat slanted over his dark face, standing at the road's edge on the outskirts of Rudioso, New Mexico.

The tangy scent of pines hung sharp as antiseptic in the high mountain air. Vince, loaded with cash, felt good after winning big on Timetothinkrich in the All-American Futurity. He was also drunk or he wouldn't have stopped, not with wads of bills stuffed in his pockets. Too satisfied with his win to care. Besides, Angel wasn't exactly a stranger. He was a horse player seen around the tracks for years.

"You didn't come up a winner," Vince said when Angel slipped in beside him.

Angel looked weary and rumpled, bits of straw clinging to him as if he'd slept in a stable. Easing back his hat, he managed a smile. "Would I hitch if I did?"

"Not likely."

"Not likely, right. Jesus, you never know when you'll take a beating. I played it safe today, kept my cool and went with the favorite, that Coca's Kid, and the son-of-bitch come up third."

Vince shook his head. "Don't want to tell you how to run your life, but that wasn't smart."

"How'd you mean?"

Driving between rows of pines, Vince took a hand from the wheel and jerked a can of beer from the open six-pack at this feet and passed another to Angel. "I'll tell you how it is. In a field of class horses you never go with the favorite. It's not worth it, working against the odds. Know what I mean? When you've got ten class horses like they had out there this afternoon, the ten best two-year-olds in the country, you know any one of them has the stuff to win. So why go for short odds when you can figure something better."

"That ain't always so easy."

"Sure it is; that's the point. You've just got to be smarter than the horses. Is that so tough? It takes brains, patience and courage. You've got to know what the hell you're doing."

They rode toward Alamogordo, Vince drinking, explaining a betting system both complex and sensible, its strengths clearly and repeatedly stated, its weaknesses vague and unformed behind a screen of words.

"That's it. I've got it all figured."

"Must be nice." Angel's voice was quiet, guarded. "I haven't had a good season in a long time."

"You going on to Prescott?"

"If that's where the horses are going."

Vince polished off his beer. The empty can sailed out the open window. "Ride with me." He felt light-headed, expansive. "I'll give you some pointers. We can figure something out."

Angel shrugged. "Sure," he said. "Why not? Who knows? Maybe we'll do each other a big favor."

Some favor, Vince thinks. Some big deal. You give a guy a lift and in the end he takes your two hundred dollars and bets on the wrong horse. Two hundred that would have won thousands, all because he thinks he knows something you don't, thinks he's smarter than you. It's what you get for picking up these weirdos, deadbeat creeps. Okay for a while, someone to talk to, keep you from getting drowsy and running off the road. Sometimes they're good for other things. Guiding the Chevy through a final rock-rimmed curve before reaching the valley floor, he remembers that Angel had run his errands, carried his beer, backed him up in barroom brawls, procured his women. But Vince is in the habit of canceling debts. He doesn't want to feel he owes anyone anything. Besides, didn't the Mexican come out ahead? He's the one who blew the two hundred, and didn't he always have an eye on Vince's women? That's what gets Vince: the duplicity. The fact you can't trust a friend.

"You going someplace to meet a girl?"

The boy's face jerks up, his eyes startled. "Huh?"

"Thought maybe you were going someplace to meet your girl."

"No. No, nothing like that. I don't have a girl. I'm only going to Yuma to see if there's work."

"Yuma, huh? Not much doing in Yuma. You should try Phoenix. There's a town that swings a little. But Yuma, I don't know. How come you haven't got a girl?"

"Huh?"

"A girl, for Christ's sake. How come you haven't got one?"

"Don't know. I was married for a while. But me and my wife separated. She said she was too young to settle down. She's seventeen. Now my Mom's stuck with raising the kid. I figured if I could get work in Yuma and rent a place, me and Wanda could get back together."

"Wanda?"

"My wife. She'll be eighteen in October."

Traveling fast, the car reaches bottom, settling against the black length of highway, a sleek animal starting its spring across the flatlands. Behind it the moon soars above the mountains. The desert lies ahead, limitless, splayed eastward like spilled ale, secretive and terrible in its emptiness. Vince stretches and yawns, then resettles behind the wheel.

"Forget her. Do yourself a favor. I had that. It isn't worth it."

"I don't know."

"Let me tell you: I've had it both ways. Some women, the minute you touch them, are ready to rent a room and run out to buy furniture and stoves and garbage disposals and crap like that. All they care about is a turkey in the oven and a man with a steady job. Others are only hot for a quick one. There's no comparison.

Listen, last night back in Del Mar, I had a little red-headed number. We didn't even take time to learn each other's names. Know what I mean?"

And so, riding across the black and undulant desert, the boy listens and gnaws his toothpick as Vince relates the story of a one-night romance, enumerating a variety of sexual possibilities, implying that in the space of a few hours and with a virtual stranger, he experienced them all. He doesn't mention that under his clothing the smell of her still clings, the smell of cheap body powder and mouthwash, the sour odor of bed sheets used by too many. The pleasure in talking slides away as he recalls the cold thrust of her spare body, the scornful set of her jaw, his own half-hearted exertions carrying him at last to a moment's flawed release.

"Soon as I get to town," he says, speeding past the turnoff into Coyote Wells service area, "soon as I get there, I've got a woman to see."

"Yeah?"

"That's why I asked if you were going to see your girl. I've got to see this woman. Only I don't know. It'll probably be the end and not the beginning."

"Everything ends sometime."

"That's exactly right. You've got to know when enough is enough. I've been with this one all summer. Some ways, it's okay. But she can't let go. Know what I mean? She's always hanging on. I go out, she's got to come along. I stay in, there she is, stretched on the bed, just asking for it. I've got no time to myself, no time to concentrate. When I go to the races, I don't even know what horses are running. How can you pick winners if you don't do your homework? How do you keep a woman when you aren't winning money to spend on her? It's a vicious circle. Know what I mean? Life is like that sometimes, a damn vicious circle."

As if life has taught him a similar lesson, the boy nods in accord, spits the nibbled toothpick onto the floor, then fishes a fresh one from his pocket. "I know what you mean."

"Sure you do. It's all part of human experience. The last time I saw her, we were in this bar. One of her old boyfriends started bothering her. I got pissed off and punched him pretty hard, broke his jaw. After that I left town. Once I got away I could think. Back at Del Mar the horses were eating out of my hand. I was winning again. Now I've got to pack my stuff, tell her I'm on my way."

"Sometimes it's the only thing you can do."

"Other times I'm not so sure. Don't get me wrong. She's okay. Likes to have a good time. And good looking, a sharp looking woman. Not like the ordinary women you see on the street, something special. Beautiful, I'd guess you'd say. You get used to something like that. You get so you like to have it around. It's not easy to give up."

"Can't be anything much harder."

"Huh?"

"Than leaving a beautiful girl. Can't be anything harder than that."

"You can say that again."

"Wanda's like that—beautiful, I mean. Never seen a girl more beautiful than her." The boy shifts his hat, sighs and jabs the toothpick at his mouth. "She's short, but not skinny. Wanda's not like one of those in fashion magazines. She's got hips and a chest. Stacked, I guess you'd say. And real dark-skinned, with brown eyes and black hair hanging down her back. Before we got married, her name was Chavez. Her mother's American, but her father's Mexican."

Vince turns and peers into the gloom beside him. "You married Mexican, huh?"

"On her father's side. Anything wrong with that?"

"What's it matter to me? It's your business. You want to marry Mexican, why should I care?"

"Half-Mexican."

"That's up to you."

"How do you mean?"

"I've had friends, Mexicans, that's all. Guys I thought I was pretty close to. But they're shifty, like people say. Always up to something. Turned out I couldn't trust them."

"We're all individuals. It's not a person's race that matters."

Vince looks at the boy as if he's never seen him before. The wind rushes past. Even so, the air in the car is stifling. Vince watches sweat bead down the boy's pinched face and suddenly feels constrained by his presence. "Some people say that, but I'm not sure. I've slept with Mexican women. More than once, too, and it was okay. When it comes to taking a man into their beds, they know what they're doing. But marrying one, I don't know."

"Seems to me if you sleep with a woman, you ought to be willing to marry her."

Mocking laughter explodes from Vince's mouth. "I thought your generation was supposed to be liberated. If I thought like you, I'd have set up some damn peculiar households. What are you, a Bible nut or something? You belong to one of these religious sects?"

The youth looks away, gazing at the passing desert. "Me? I only know what I think."

"Well, you've got some damned funny opinions."

"I only know."

The boy's voice is barely audible. Vince feels him turn, shutting himself away, sullen, withdrawn. The car rolls on, two miles; the unchanging desert flashes past though now the air carries the distant smell of water. Before long they'll reach the first canals, the blackness of irrigated fields.

The Chevy slows, stoplights flaring behind, then bumps to a

halt on the gravel shoulder. Darkness settles like a leaden mold.

"Shit! Feels like a flat."

"A flat?"

"Flat tire. Feels like the right rear's gone flat. Jump out and have a look."

The boy steps out. In the soft light from the interior, he bends, a hand resting on the open door. "Looks okay to me."

"Must be the left rear. Cross around and check."

The door slams and Vince sees the boy move through the flare of taillights. Vince waits. A smile touches his mouth as he counts slowly under his breath, hands composed around the steering wheel, eyes fixed on the rearview mirror. He counts to three, four, five until he's sure the boy is bent over the tire. Then, with a sudden jerk, he slams his foot on the gas. The Chevy guns forward. An abrupt rattle of gravel rains in the fender wells, a sharp bite of rubber on asphalt, and Vince is away.

"Fucking weirdo!"

A hundred yards down the road the car slues to a stop. The boy's canvas duffel tumbles into a ditch.

FRENCH LETTERS

Max's head bobs like a crappie float as he shuffles toward the mess on the driveway. Smack in the middle. Plain as day. Trash, real filth. Hard to believe. He's had trouble before, plenty of it, but nothing like this. Stooping, he peers down. Birds squabble overhead, sparrows swooping toward the feeder next door. Max doesn't notice. Puffing heavily, hands on knees, he lowers himself. "Should have expected this," he mutters. "The world being what it is."

Sun brightens the yard. Morning sun angling sharply over Ajay's elm and across Honey Lane, lighting Max's pampered lawn and clipped hedge, the whitewashed cobblestones bordering the walk. It beats full on his back but fails to warm him.

In jockey shorts and singlet he stares at the pile of debris. Cigarette butts lie mounded between his slippers. A few cork tips scattered here and there, cork tips stained with slashes of lipstick the color of tangerines. Ashes, too, ashes and candy wrappers and a wad of soot-covered gum. But it's the tangerine lipstick that gets Max. What kind of woman would wear something like that?

For a moment he thinks he'll call the police. When Peggy was alive they called the police pretty often. Her health was bad and Max had to look out for her.

They moved here after Max Jr. was killed in Korea, on the road from Inchon Reservoir. He was part of the retreat. Every month that winter Peggy mailed him a quart can of fruit juice to keep up his strength. First, she doctored the can, extracted the juice through a tiny hole she drilled in the bottom, replaced the juice with brandy, sealed the hole with a dab of solder. Peggy's idea. She spent hours in the kitchenette of their Third St. apartment, wielding a hypodermic syringe, swapping alcohol for juice. She hoped to save her son from freezing in the Korean winter. Instead he was incinerated when his armored personnel carrier took a hit from antitank fire. There wasn't enough left of him to send home. The last can of smuggled brandy came back to Third St., the package stamped: *Return to Sender*.

Max bought the house on Honey Lane, hoping it would pull Peggy out of her decline. He worked at Piggly Wiggly while Peggy hustled part-time for the Welcome Wagon. The depth of her despair was bottomless. When she had nothing left to give to the memory of her son, she started on herself. First, her gall bladder, then a kidney. Half a lung. A tumor on her womb. At the mental health clinic on Haskell St., a cool young psychologist informed her that she hated her body so much she wanted bits and pieces cut off whenever she felt particularly blue. Peggy didn't argue. It wasn't long before she had open-heart surgery, then the stroke that paralyzed and took her.

With Peggy in the care of doctors, Max spent his time whitewashing the cobblestones edging his walks, laying out the 90 millimeter shell casings bordering the flowerbeds, marking his possessions with plastic tags: Private Property of Max Fowler. Sometimes, when he had nothing to do and Peggy was stretched in the darkened bedroom with a damp towel on her head, he went down the block to visit the neighbors.

Things were different in those days. He knew everyone up and down the block: the Lynds, Fullers, Jones, the Waldos. They all moved in when the tract opened, helped each other when help was needed, kept to themselves when it wasn't. They built rumpus rooms, planted hedges, kept their cars clean and lawns mown. Standing out by his mailbox, Max saw Airstream trailers parked in driveways and Old Glory run up flagpoles.

The neighbors slowly vanished. Sirened away to Pleasure Acres or Leisure World. The Waldos went to Canada, Judy and Ed Murry bought a trailer and had it towed to Lawrence Welk's Champagne Mobile Home Park in California. Abandoned, Max resented the departures, despised the Christmas cards with the inevitable Polaroid snaps of sunburned jowls pendulous beneath baseball caps. He stalked the neighborhood on the lookout for someone he knew. Of the old crowd only the Jessups remained. He still saw Earl beside his big, blue hydrangea bush, a deathgrip on his chromium walker, gazing blankly into the distance as if dropped from a UFO.

Even if he were in Ga-Ga-Land, Old Earl was better than the new breed, with names you couldn't pronounce. They were forever playing stereos and TVs at all hours, throwing parties, parking motorcycles and pick-ups in front of his house. When something like that happened Max put in a call. He was pretty well known. "Okay, Mr. Fowler, we'll take care of it." That was the line the cops always took. More often than not, they did nothing. The music blared; the parties roared.

When Peggy's brain short-circuited the final time, Max was left alone in the medicinal stink and unused rooms. It was then he took things into his own hands. Telephoning the noisemakers, he told them to pipe down. Ridicule was all he got. He was a man robbed of his son, cheated by his wife's illness of the kind of life a man ought to have, and now a victim of that final creeping impediment: old age. These young people had everything: fast cars and dancing to all hours, chasing sex and dollars and cheap thrills, low-lifes who wouldn't give the time of day to a shuffling old widower. Some turned up the volume when he called. The airline stewardesses across the street—cheap blondes who sunbathed practically naked on their front lawn—turned up their stereo so it sounded like the Aurora High Marching Band quick stepping down Honey Lane.

When the phone calls got him nowhere, he slipped out the back door and canvassed the neighborhood. The first few evenings he did nothing more than let the air out of tires. Crouched at the curb, he pressed in valve stems and smelled the warm rubbery air hissing into the night. Later, he slashed tires, snapped antennas, rammed a screwdriver through tinted windshields.

Somebody got wise. He never knew who but figured it was Al Valerian, the delivery driver who lived two doors up from the blondes. He had no reason to suspect Valerian except that one night, not far from his door, Max was struck by a large, wet dog spiral. When he wiped away the mess, no one was around. The lights were out in Valerian's house though from inside, Max was sure he heard laughter.

He grew more determined. Creeping behind the Spargo's house during one of their free-for-all parties, he clipped their electric lines with his pole pruner and was home in front of the tv while they hollered for candles. With the blondes on a flight over the Pacific, he broke a pane in their basement window, rammed in their garden hose and left the water running. His favorite prank was pouring a pound of sugar into the gas tank of Valerian's delivery van. With a grin of satisfaction he watched it start the next morning and vanish up the block. It never came back. "Keep the damn thing off the streets," he told himself. "Keep the streets free of this foreign garbage."

When the bombings began, the Valerians were out of town.

Max didn't know who to blame. The charge was so small Max thought it was a truck backfiring and went back to sleep. Next morning he found the door of his mailbox lying in the gutter. He had built the box himself. A replica of his house, it was exact, right down to the weather vane and apple-green shutters. On the blown-off door glimmered a miniature brass knob and a small window with four plexiglass panes. He held the door to his nose and sniffed cordite. A policeman came, jotted something in a notebook and drove away. With paint and a new hinge, Max repaired the mailbox on its pole beside the curb. Afterward, he put his tools away and went inside to watch *The Young and the Restless*.

On Halloween dynamite ripped the mailbox from its post, hurling it down the block. This time Max rebuilt with brick and mortar. Within a week it was reduced to rubble. Max was asleep in a recliner pulled close to the window, a .22 automatic clutched in his fist, when the blast hit the room. The sappers had rushed the box, placed the charge, then raced away before Max knew what happened. Bricks rained down as, pistol ready, he rushed into the yard.

This time the cop got out of his car, poked through debris and made notes before driving away. Max didn't expect him to solve the crime. He wasn't disappointed. Life was nothing but slow disaster.

In the end Max built a portable mailbox, carrying it to the curb each afternoon to watch the postman slip in wads of circulars, fourth-class advertising and bills. Then Max dragged it inside to see if anyone had written.

With the mailbox no longer a target, his peonies were torched, his whitewashed cobblestones splashed with blood-red paint. Once, someone poured salt in a pattern on his manicured lawn. When the grass died there were four letters in brown spelling a word poor Peggy, God-rest-her-soul, wouldn't have recognized.

Now this. Trash strewn across his driveway. The contents of an ashtray, a litter bag and wads of Kleenex drifting into the flower beds. Down the drive a puddle of oil seeped into the pale, carefully swept concrete. Someone parked there and dumped their garbage. Acid churned around the nub of Max's ulcer.

If Peggy were alive he wouldn't tell her of this latest outrage. At the end, the least thing had her in tears: an obscene phone call, kids ringing the bell and running. When she saw Max crossing the lawn in undershorts, she closed the curtains, stretched out on her recliner and lay in darkness, tears tracking the throat of her robe. He couldn't understand why. Was she siding with the neighbors? Sometimes he thought so. What did it matter if he wore his underwear in public? Who knew the difference between jockey shorts and bathing trunks? Not even the cop who showed up one day claiming someone had reported a case of indecent exposure.

He begins cleaning. In the garage, behind his '62 Buick, he finds broom, dustpan, a plastic trash bucket mounted on wheels. He sweeps up the mess, then spreads kitty litter on the oil, standing back to admire his work.

Then he spots it—farther down the drive. Concentrated on Kleenex, cigarette butts and oil, he missed it. There it lies: a transparent, sluglike sheath stiffening in the morning sun. He stares in disbelief. Stooping over the thing, he tries to remember what it's called. It's been a long time. Too long. "A fishskin," he says aloud, trying out the word as though it were foreign. "No. A French letter. That's it. A goddamn French letter."

Foil glitters at the edge of the grass. Max examines it. "Sensi-tip," he reads. "Extra Thin and Fully Lubricated—For that Special Feeling. Nothing Between You and Your Loved One." A clear, jellylike fluid oozes from the corner where the foil is torn.

After wrapping the French letter in a wad of paper, he flushes it down the toilet. Standing above the bowl, he watches the water swirl, the paper sucked straight down. Blindly, he stares into the bathroom mirror, thinking only of tangerine lipstick, the woman who wears it. That thing was in her. Slipped right inside.

Hose in hand he washes down the drive. Furiously, he sprays until the gutter is full. Water flows down the block and into the storm drain on the next street.

Mornings he searches the drive, now wearing dark gabardine slacks and one of Max Jr.'s sport shirts. They hang by the dozen under plastic covers in the spare room. When Peggy was alive he never touched Maxie's clothes. Though they pinch under the arms and the buttons won't close, they give him a feeling of confidence, as if beneath the loud check and tropical swirls is a body that can cope with the world.

Walking Honey Lane, in the supermarket, sitting on a bench in Danforth Plaza, he examines the faces of passing women. Sooner or later he'll find her, the one with tangerine lips. At first he thinks it's Mona, the Valerian girl. Fourteen or fifteen, baby fat stretching the front of her too tight T-shirts and packing the seat of her too tight jeans, she struts the block in front of Max's house. His gaze follows her through a gap in the blinds. Stepping through a side door, he approaches her across the lawn. Makeup is piled on thick and a tangle of golden curls bounces on her head. Through her T-shirt the dark impress of nipples. He draws a deep breath. Mona is just the sort of tramp he would suspect. He closes in for a better look. She glances in his direction, cigarette clinging to her lip, and blows a smoke ring as if offering a gift—dense, round, perfectly formed. He feels a warm stirring he can't deny. The smoke ring hangs between them, dissolves at its center as Max sees the girl's cool eyes ice right through him. Twitching her rear, she parades off down the block. But not before he gets a good look at her pouting mouth. The lipstick is all wrong, much too deep, too red. No, not red: purple-black like a bruise.

The stewardesses, those two hot-looking blondes, wear pale

pink stuff that makes them look as if they have pernicious anemia. On the street, under the potted trees at Aurora Mall, Max's eyes shift from face to face.

At last he finds it at Tru-Drugs. The rack displays dozens of colors. He glances round, no one watching. The tube is cool as an old coin in his hand. He peers closely. Nights in the Gardens of Spain.

"May I help you?"

The salesgirl is Asian, probably a refugee. She's tiny, with dark, heavily made-up eyes, hair black as patent leather, and bones fine as a bird's. Max's breath catches in his throat. He could crush her in his hands.

"I'd like this for my wife."

"Anything else?" She doesn't smile. He leans forward, gazes at the fragile wings of her collar bones under skin fine as sunlight, the minute bones of her chest vanishing like a zipper into the opening of her blouse.

"What I wanted—aaah, I'm not sure it's the right color." His eyes meet the girl's, then dart away. "Maybe if you could try."

Laying the tube in her hand he watches her remove the cap. The lipstick slips into view, wet, slick and shiny as all the peters on all the dogs that ever tore through the garden when Ginger, Peggy's Cocker Spaniel, was in heat.

Jesus Christ! What made him think of that? Is he crazy? All these years he's had nothing. Nothing. He's an old man. Yet he can only think of that something to fill the nothing.

"Something," he says.

The girl looks up, a fine crease delineating deep eyes. "Pardon?"

"Nothing. Nothing, really."

The girl's face tips forward. Blinking dizzily, Max watches her draw a slash of tangerine across the small bulge of paper-colored skin where her thumb and index finger join. Like an open wound.

She lifts her hand for inspection. It smells of cologne and fresh fruit and the girl's immaculate skin. Urgently, he grasps her fingers. The color is exactly right.

Nights in the Gardens of Spain lies on the table beside his bed. Max lifts the cap and screws the lipstick into position. Sometimes, with his face pressed close to the mirror and his mouth twisted into a feminine smirk, he colors his lips thick with the stuff. The fragrance, the taste, the breath that come back to him from the glass are charged with a power he neither understands nor tries to explain.

The morning arrives when he finds the refuse where it lay before. Camel butts—shreds of dark tobacco spilling from crushed paper. Candy wrappers, wads of gum. Three cork-tipped cigarette ends smeared with tangerine. One is quite long. Max studies it. The imprint of the woman's lips is perfectly clear. He makes out the lines and whorls, the narrow indentations and wonders if, like fingerprints, the pressure of a woman's mouth can give her away.

Bathed in a puddle of its own, the French letter lies further down the drive. Lifting it carefully, Max lays it across his palm. Wet and sticky with fluids he cannot let himself imagine. His eyes blur. Smelling of rubber and a lingering faraway odor of the sea, the French letter swims in its juices. He peers at it. Sniffs. Closes his eyes. As if it were an oyster lying on the half shell of his hand, he slips it into his mouth, feels it slide down his throat.

It's cold. The numbness in his toes works up his ankles. Age, he thinks. Circulation about shot. He wraps the flaps of his robe around his knees. He'll wait five minutes, then go in. Through the open door wind blasts across a black sky, a moving tide sweeping down from the north. Branches scratch the garage wall; leaves clatter over the roof and across the drive. Five minutes more. Five minutes, just for luck.

When he wakes he's stiff with cold, frozen, his robe worked up around his thighs and open across his chest. How long did he sleep? The wind has died and the leaves no longer make a racket. But he hears a sound, the sound of a car slowing in front of the house.

Police patrol or somebody coming home from a party. Still, he's tense as he eases up in the Buick and peers through the loop of the steering wheel.

A pale car, one of those foreign models, a Mazda or Toyota, stops in front of the house. The lights blink off, then on again, and finally blink off for good. This is it. The car backs up the drive, brake lights flaring in the cold as it stops. "Holy Jesus," Max whispers. "It's her."

He waits. He's gone over this a hundred times in his mind. Step by step. The first kiss. Knuckles kneading breasts. Zippers working down. Give them time. Plenty of time. Slowly, very slowly. He begins counting: "One-thousand-and-one, one-thous-and-and-two, one-thousand-and-three . . . ." He longs to leap from the car, rush down the drive. Longs for it to begin. To end. The cold forgotten, sweat beads on his forehead, springs deep in his armpits. "One-thousand-and-eight, one-thousand-and-nine . . . ."

The Buick's door opens without a sound. Max always liked a big, solid car. He keeps the hinges soft with grease. Weeks ago he unscrewed the bulb from the interior light. Blindly, he feels his way along a fender and steps from the cover of the garage. A sliver of moon, pale and distant, rests beyond Ajay's elm. The streetlight shines dimly down the block.

He takes a breath, releasing it slowly. Thick hands hang loosely at his sides, heavy and numb as if wearing cotton gloves. His bare feet skate numbly over smooth concrete, the .22 automatic riding the pocket of his robe.

He makes out the pyracantha, clusters of berries dark in the November chill; wind-topped chrysanthemums, green coils of garden hose like an African snake. A gust of wind opens his robe, swirls the hem to his hips, then abruptly dies. He feels the pistol's heft—the pistol and the raw edge of a car's bumper against his legs.

He imagines the scene: dark hair against pale shoulders, clothes tossed onto the backseat. It happened on this driveway; it happened in his imagination. It's happening now.

Side-stepping, he edges across the rear of the car, rounds the fender and starts toward the front. His robe brushes the surface, his body touching mud-spattered paint. Easy, he tells himself. Easy. In a minute it will begin. And end.

Halfway to the door, headlights sweep out of Vintage Circle onto Honey Lane, track across the grass and catch Max. He freezes. It's going wrong, all wrong. His whole life nothing but one wrong turn after another. Nothing working. Nothing.

His eyes close as he takes a breath. "One-thousand-and-one." The car passes and stops in front of the Valerians. Mona coming home from a date. Lights snap off but no one gets out. It'll be parked there till dawn. With a slut like Mona, till dawn or longer. Max will think about Mona later, deal with her another time. Now he will do what he must.

Reaching the door, he peers through the glass. The luminescence of human flesh startles him—the poignancy in the juxtaposition of bodies, their deep, slow rhythms. A vulnerability in the milky tuck and flair of waist, hips and thighs, the extraordinary fall of a breast overwhelm him.

His eyes fill with tears. He longs for her to turn, to see her face, the raw tangerine lipstick streaking her mouth. He aches for her. Needs her to see the tears tracking his face. But she only rocks slowly backward and forward, backward and forward.

Wiping his eyes Max stands transfixed. When he reaches for the door, the chromium handle is ice under his touch.

THE CLOSER

Dizzy with arrogance, seduced by power, Il Duce mounted his *Palazzo Venezia* balcony each day that spring between the wars to bray at the Fascist donkeys crowding the piazza below. He harangued, cajoled, hammered a breast barnacled in medals. And on a sparkling morning late in May, at the dictator's command, Italian trains truly ran on time. Even Eduardo Volpe, skeptic, scholar, aesthete, renowned spelunker in the deep cave of the Italian Renaissance, was inspired by this last impossible accomplishment. From the terrace of his hillside villa he gazed over fields, olive groves and vineyards to the towers and domes of Florence rising through blue mist in the valley below, thinking that that *stronzo* Mussolini might not be such a bad egg after all.

Volpe was barely five feet tall, with a slight build and delicate features. His deep brown eyes were large. His nose straight and long. His fleshy upper lip revealed a sensuousness the rest of his bony aristocratic head belied. As if to conceal what some believed a sign of his profligacy, he wore a neatly trimmed mustache and spade-shaped beard that over the years turned as white as the linen suits he habitually wore.

These suits were not the damp, tropical, capacious variety worn by Sidney Greenstreet as he lounged sinisterly in exotic films. But Savile Row creations, their impeccably cut, narrow-shouldered jackets nipped in at the waist, buttoned thrice over belly-hugging vests, while snug trousers flared at the knees and fell copiously over shoes of white patent leather. You had the notion that dozens of laundresses stood just offstage, washing, bleaching and pressing to keep the Professor at his snowy sartorial zenith. The only accent was a scarlet carnation, snipped early that morning by Pippo, the villa's gardener, and worn like a bullet wound in the Professor's narrow lapel.

White and impossibly clean, he stepped excitedly from one end of the long terrace to the other, his shoes snapping sharply over the old stones. His habit was to walk here each morning, admiring his forty acres of olive trees, at this season their silvery branches thick with tiny ivory blossoms promising rows of demijohns filled with golden olive oil when the harvesting and pressing were finished the week before Christmas. In the vineyards below the olives, shoots emerged from gnarled vines and the first green runners advanced along lattices. Homegrown oil. Chianti from the villa's cellar. Cucumbers, *melanzane*, crisp green lettuce, glowing tomatoes red as cardinals' hats, fresh from the kitchen garden. Though he ate little himself the Professor took pleasure in the table he set with the abundance of his land. Each day a dozen guests joined him in the grand *sala da pranzo*, Signora Volpe at the foot of the long table, the Professor at its head, Milena and Gabriella serving the dishes Gino prepared in the huge, smoky, vaulted kitchen. Platters and bowls of *gnocchi verdi*, *zuppa di ceci*, *panzanella*, *saltimbocca* pungent with truffles.

Among the twelve apostles who came to the villa each noon, there were always a few new faces as well as veterans of the social wars, scholars, film stars, diplomats and politicians, an occasional poet, always a novelist, frequently a prince or princess, aristocrats from Italy, mannequins from France, art dealers from England, millionaires from America. An invitation to lunch at the villa was as sought after in Florence as seats at the *Follies Bergere* in Paris. In its way it was a floorshow, a cultural extravaganza, the true purpose of which, figuratively at least, was to allow these dozen diners to sit spellbound and reverential at the Professor's small, white-shod feet.

Hostesses, cab drivers, desk clerks, waiters saw to it that those still innocent of the story when their invitations arrived learned the details before reaching the gates and ascending the villa's cypress-lined drive. It was straightforward in the extreme.

Born Teddy Fox in the Lewis and Clark country of northern Idaho, the Professor was the only child of a hardworking mining engineer and his beautiful, much younger wife, a fey, raven-haired theosophist who gave piano lessons to Teddy's schoolmates in the candlelit parlor each afternoon, and with feverish skill played Couperin suites through the long polar nights. With money inherited from a saloon-keeping uncle, a notorious swindler who, in the days of the Mother Lode, promoted bare-knuckled prize fights, bear baiting and prostitution in the back room and cardsharps and boozers out front, Teddy's mother sent the boy away when he was old enough to travel alone. She envisioned a world beyond the mining camps of the Coeur d'Alene and longed for Teddy to enter it. He went first to Choate, then Yale and finally Oxford. Had he stayed home, a runt with an oversized brain, no athletic pretensions and a hatred of the wilder aspects of the great outdoors, who knows what sort of brutal rednecked manipulator and country thug he might have become? In the green fields of academe, however, he grew intellectually fat, and in his final year at Yale, following a summer in Italy, he had written his still highly-regarded critical gem: *Sienese Masters*. In it he revealed a new aesthetic, a profound, uncluttered view of the works of Duccio di

Bouninsegna, Simone Martini, Pietro and Ambrogio Lorenzetti. Following *Sienese Masters*, a new book appeared almost yearly with Eduardo Volpe's name on the spine: *Study and Criticism of Renaissance Art*; *Piero della Francesca*; *Painters of the Italian Renaissance*. His masterpiece, *Masaccio: Creation of an Aesthetic*, secured his reputation that, in turn, kept his lucrative trade in "attributions" humming and his luncheon table crowded with a polyglot crew of highbrow celebrities.

He seldom bothered with the guest list so long as homage was paid. Selecting a lively clutch of invitees was the responsibility of his secretary, Clarice dé Benci, and Signora Volpe. An educated Iowa farmgirl who hid her native wit and intellectual gifts behind a massive matronly facade, the Signora managed the practical side of running the villa while Clarice, a willowy dark-haired Tuscan whose beauty might have inspired Botticelli and was young enough to be the Professor's granddaughter, cared for the creative. Two rumors in particular circulated about these women. The first, that Signora Volpe had taken the Professor's raw ideas and crafted the exquisite prose that characterized his books. She was a student at Swarthmore when they met at a symposium on the pre-Raphaelites, the year before Volpe's first Italian journey. They formed an early and lasting attachment, he attracted largely by her practical nature and the lucid prose of the letters she wrote him daily, she by his astuteness and the raw desire to attain what he called "a level." Had she written the books? It seems unlikely. Although the possibility exists that there was a collaboration, a meeting of minds, a conversation of sorts between co-creators that resulted in the illumination of a radiant moment in our generally dim history.

Almost too obvious to mention, the second rumor linked the Professor and Clarice in a love affair. The Professor was noted for his *affaires de coeur*. It was understood. A beefy, good-natured woman with the practical inclinations of a farm wife, the

Signora had no desire and little time for the entanglements of the boudoir. She left the entertainment of the Professor's person to the stray finches and fluttering pigeons who swooped about him. If Clarice was among the Professor's birds, so much the better as far as the Signora was concerned. As bright as she was astonishingly beautiful, Clarice kept the Professor content and at least some starlings out of the nest.

After pacing the terrace from end to end, the Professor entered the library through French doors. Row upon row of leather-bound books lined the walls, and paintings, stacks of antique canvases, leaned haphazardly against walnut wainscoting. A partners' desk deep in papers, books and photographs stood at the room's center and in the gloom at the far end, on a massive bruise-colored leather couch, reclined Clarice dé Benci, a smile touching her heartbreaking mouth as she awaited her first assignment.

The spring freshness entered the open door. From the drive came a hoopoe's wild cry and from the fields workers' shouts as they spaded the earth under the olive trees. Soon the Professor's voice was heard deep in the library gloom and, from time to time above the drone, the treble of Clarice's laughter.

At exactly eleven the Professor called Pippo in from the garden. He had been trimming the ilex hedges and leaves stuck at angles from his graying hair. Little taller than the Professor and as lithe, he possessed the clever eyes and sly smile of a village Pan. While Clarice went to the kitchen the Professor gave Pippo his orders. Often the Professor called him here to move paintings. One by one the gardener lifted canvases from against the wall and, while Clarice made careful notes, the Professor made his attributions. Caravaggio. Berruguete. School of Ghirlandaio. From museums, art schools, dealers, patrons of the arts, paintings arrived at the villa for the Professor's seal of approval. If he had the least doubt, he called for the Signora to examine a picture and give her expert advice before pronouncing it either genuine or fake, a Leonardo or a Lorenzo Lotto.

This morning six pictures were to be moved, four small canvases and two panels bearing large figures. Before Pippo began Clarice returned with coffee, three small cups on a wooden tray, which they quickly drained without sitting. Then Pippo lifted the smallest of the pictures, a portrait of an overweight blonde bejewelled at the throat that the Professor, some years before and in writing, had dubbed "Swine with Pearls." "In the style of Giorgione," he had written, "but not by an astute pupil, probably painted sometime after the Master's death." Circumstances had made him reassess his judgment. He grimaced as Pippo carried the painting from the library across the *ingresso* and into the drawing room, where he placed it on an easel at the far end of the long room. Next came an Antonello da Messina portrait, an obvious forgery, the subject, Vincenzo da Pozzo, a young aristocrat born after the painter's lifetime.

One after another Pippo carried these fakes, patched and repainted frauds, these weak sisters of the fine arts, into the drawing room and arranged them in a semicircle around a burgundy and golden Bakhtiari carpet worth more than all the paintings combined. Resting on a priceless Sienese wedding chest was the centerpiece, a putative Paolo Veronese, "The Miracle of the Loaves and Fishes," picturing a banquet attended by swarms of guests, dogs, dwarfs, soldiers, a fool dining grandly beneath a classical loggia. A pastiche, in other words, of Veronese themes, painted in flashy colors with clumsy displays of foreshortening and *trompe l'oeil*. As early as 1917 the Professor declared the "Veronese" a fake, at best attributable to a follower of the artist. He damned it repeatedly in the next few years and for a time it had mercifully disappeared from the art market. Now it had resurfaced—here at the villa. He turned his back in disgust and gazed into the sunshine.

At noon Vincent Koenig arrived by taxi from his hotel in town and joined the Professor in the library. Clarice vanished and the two men sat opposite one another at the partners' desk. With his sleek hair and tidy mustache, Koenig had the reassuring good looks of an insurance executive.

"The stage is set?" Light from the French doors shone on Koenig's steel-rimmed spectacles.

The Professor sighed. "It seems overdone."

"I know my man. He enjoys a circus, a few clowns tossing tenpins."

"These are trained elephants, I fear built of *papier-mâché*."

"My dear Volpe, excepting the Veronese, Madison has seen these pictures and wants to buy. All you need do is hold his hand and reassure him. Tell him they're the genuine thing, the valuable item. He's a simple man who enjoys a game like any child, especially an American child."

"You forget, I know something of American children myself. We are not all fools—evidence to the contrary. Besides, the man is a millionaire, a shark feeding among capitalist barracudas. He can't be a total innocent."

"But, Volpe, you and I are not capitalist barracudas. We are not at sea. We have him on our ground here."

"The high ground?"

"*Esatto, amico mio.*" Koenig laughed and clapped his hands. Sunlight glancing wildly from his glasses nearly blinded the Professor. "The Veronese alone will have him in ecstasy. It is a masterpiece, don't you agree? Crawford's done another smashing job. The overpainting is admirable, the retouching superb."

Walter Crawford was chief restorer at Koenig's London gallery. The Professor winced at the mention of his name. "Crawford is a butcher," he said. "The Veronese is trash but it looked a good deal more like a Veronese before Crawford worked it over."

"Surely, Volpe, you can give our friend Madison a more

enlightened view." Koenig cocked his head toward the terrace. "I think I hear him arriving. I hired a Rolls and sent it by his hotel."

"I would think the man could afford his own Rolls."

"Just the sort you provide one for. Boxes of the best cigars waiting in hotel rooms along his journey. The correct scents of cologne and toilet soap. Tickets to the races and shows. My man Mackenzie pried a world of information from Madison's butler: all the man's desires."

"Pried? I'm certain you mean bought."

"An investment, Volpe, which will yield a handsome return. You won't object to splitting a few million, will you, old boy? Play your part and the man will be clay in our hands. But come, your guests have arrived." The men stood and crossed the room. At the door Koenig laid a hand on the Professor's shoulder. "By the way, his daughter is traveling with him." Koenig opened the door and ushered the Professor into the *ingresso*. "She'll set you up, old man."

Her name was Rose and she was most attractive. At least the Professor found her so. A tall, blue-eyed girl in her twenties, with dimples, blonde hair clipped short as a boy's, and a small mouth painted scarlet like a rosebud. Seated on the Professor's right, she entertained him with a spirited stream of stories of her beaus back home, fun-loving American boys with fast cars, hip flasks and a passion for all-night dancing. When she laughed, a high trilling song like a bird's, the Professor folded his hands in his lap and leaned close to see the flash of her small, white, even teeth, the pink lick of her tongue.

The real center of interest, however, lay at the opposite end of the table, and the Professor was not so smitten by the daughter that he failed to keep an eye on the father. Madison sat at Signora Volpe's right, Clarice across from him. He was a large man, thick through the middle, with a great slab-like head supporting broad, pendulous ears of such scope they reminded the Professor of his remark to Koenig about elephants. Though Madison's huge skull dwarfed his gray eyes, his gaze was clear and direct, even if it lacked what the Professor called "penetration."

His voice did not lack penetration. Above the daughter's babbling the Professor clearly heard Madison boast, in language rich with Chicago idioms, of the millions he'd made in the elevator and milling business. He had a loaf of bread for a heart, flour flowed in his veins. He had no time for "nuances," he claimed. He lived life in one dimension, one direction only: "Full speed ahead!"

Clearly taken with Clarice's beauty and the Signora's gentle questioning, Madison was in the full throes of oratory. Now that he'd made more money than one man could possibly spend, he explained, it was time to spread himself a little, to look into some corners he'd bypassed in his race for the dollar. The accumulation of capital had a price, a price he was no longer willing to pay. Besides, he had a loving daughter, a wonderful wife too delicate for travel. He owed it to them to bring something of the larger world into their lives.

Down the table the Professor saw Koenig, placed where he could keep an eye on the proceedings, change the direction if he saw things veer off-course, rubbing his hands together. Things were going, as young Rose might have put it, swimmingly. Even her incessant babble had a certain musical quality, like a nonsense aria sung in a language no one understood. On the Professor's left the novelist, a sharp-faced woman whose recent book the Professor had no intention of reading, had given up trying to gain his attention and found that she and the plump young poet across from her had a common interest in gardening. From time to time conversation became general. Inevitably, they discussed Mussolini. Praised for "shaping up" the Italians, draining the Pontine Marshes, making the trains run on time; damned for the *mezzadria*, the new economic scheme giving greater rewards to tenant farmers. The Professor complained of the coming ruination of the "landed classes," but before his roar grew too loud the proximity of Rose's dimples distracted him. Once more everyone fell happily into conversation with those nearby. The food was excellent—Gino's wild asparagus tossed with fresh fettuccine followed by his truffle-rich *saltimbocca*. Milena and Gabriella kept everyone's glass topped with a vintage Chianti brought up from the cellar for the occasion.

However, things were not perfect in the Professor's social paradise. First, the dreaded moment of "attribution" was approaching and though Clarice, Koenig and Signora Volpe were putting Madison in a mood where he might buy the Brooklyn Bridge, it was not a bridge the Professor wished to sell. Secondly, he was unhappy to discover Geoffrey Bliss roosting at mid-table, spooning up Gino's *Monte Bianco* as if he hadn't eaten in months, though several splotches on his offensive tie were as fresh as last night's lasagna. A large man with the head and body of a whale, Bliss was a British Academy scholar who lived in a rented room above a furniture-refinishing shop on the banks of the Arno and took his meals in a grubby *trattoria* on the *Via dei Neri*. Since anyone could remember he'd been cataloguing the works of art destroyed in Savonarola's Bonfire of the Vanities. A mysterious endeavor that he believed entitled him to superior airs, a reputation for integrity, and a vicious tongue. The Professor loathed him. But Clarice had taken Bliss on as a cause, as if she hoped to civilize him. Despite the Professor's complaints Bliss was repeatedly found gorging on Gino's good cooking.

After lunch the Signora had coffee served on the terrace—a ritual finale. It wasn't long before guests gathered their wraps and made their exits. An invitation to lunch at the villa did not mean one was to spend the long silvery afternoon gossiping above the Professor's olive groves. When the last car, save Madison's Rolls, wound down the drive and passed beyond the porter's lodge, the Professor escorted the millionaire and his daughter into the drawing room. Koenig had excused himself to walk through the grounds, the Signora was in the kitchen counting spoons, and Clarice had vanished after lunch. They'd played the overture. Now it was the Professor's show.

It *was* to have been his. However, when he followed Rose and Madison into the drawing room, he discovered Geoffrey Bliss hovering like a cetaceous horror. Bliss turned as a walrus might in an ice hole, blowing and puffing, and offered the trio a whalelike grin. The man's tie boiled, the Professor noted, would make a passable minestrone.

"This," the Professor explained dryly, "is to be a private viewing."

"All apologies, my dear Volpe." Bliss's grin swelled as he spoke. His voice rose and fell in an unhinging recitative. "Looking for the loo when I discovered these dee-licious pictures. My dear, you must forgive me but I simply had to have a peek. They are scrumptious, are they not? Besides, I missed my ride back to town. Thought I might ask Madison here for a lift. That is if Miss Madison doesn't mind."

At this, Bliss's perfectly round left eye fell shut in what the Professor believed to be the most obscene wink he had ever witnessed. To his horror, Rose winked back.

"Lifts to town aside," the Professor said, "This is still a private showing."

"Not at all." Madison bowed. "That is, if you have no objection, Professor, I'd be much obliged to hear Bliss's opinion."

Was the Professor in the midst of his own worst nightmare? Bliss, of all people, horning in on this wretched business. Instinct told him to bolt and let Koenig sort out the mess. But he was not a man to let instinct rule. Especially where money was concerned. Though he was sure Bliss wished to make a fool of him, he turned to Madison and bowed stiffly. "Whatever you wish." Then, approaching the nearest picture, Giorgione's "Swine with Pearls," he began: "Once a prized possession of the Count of Ravensberg and painted at the height of Giorgione's creativity, this small portrait . . ."

"A delicious tart, wouldn't you say, Miss Madison?" Bliss interrupted, fat arms finning at his sides. "Positively delectable. Good enough to eat. Tarts this sweet are a dime-a-dozen after dark along the river, the *Lungarno Amerigo Vespucci*, only they aren't always tarts, if you get my drift."

Rose's high liquid laughter sang above her father's guffaw. The Professor looked down his patrician nose to see Bliss blush.

"Naughty again, Volpe. Most regrettable behavior. That capital Chianti of yours, I should think. Won't happen again, I assure you." Bliss turned his grin on Madison. "Volpe's the maestro here. The very best. He taught us all to see again, to feel with our eyes. Masaccio. Piero. Bellini. They'd still be locked in the dark without Volpe. We'd be drooling over the pearly flesh and nasty pink petticoats of Francois Boucher and Jean-Honore Fraggonard, certain we'd climbed to the very pinnacle of culture. Not so. Volpe showed us that. Now, we must pay close attention. The maestro has much to tell us, I'm sure, about this perfectly sumptuous Veronese. And the Antonello da Messina— I haven't seen that little wonder in ducks' years."

What was Bliss's game? Had Koenig planted a shill? Bliss knew as well as the Professor that these paintings were third-rate. Yet, his speech over, he beached himself in an armchair, propped his elbows on his knees, rested his head on his hands, prepared to absorb the Professor's wisdom.

His interest was short-lived. Before the Professor was more than a few sentences into his explication of "The Miracle of the Loaves and Fishes," Bliss began a deep-sea snore that set both Rose and her father giggling. The Professor ignored them and continued, his voice chill, rattling in his throat like leaves scudding across the drive. Somehow, he must get this ordeal behind him.

He spoke of the Veronese, then turned to the da Messina portrait of Vincenzo da Pozzo, describing it in terms of "magisterial works —indisputably autographed and in exceptional condition." When possible, he drew upon the aristocracy to make his case: "The painting under consideration, once held in the collection of Count Carlo Alfieri, was acquired from the estate of Princess Gertrude of Bad Hofgastein."

Madison nodded gravely as the aristocrats piled up. Like many Americans, like the Professor himself, if the truth were known, he was enamored with titles. In the presence of a reigning monarch, and of a very small country at that, he had fallen worshipfully to his knees and kissed the personage's quite ordinary shoe.

The Professor knew the story, Koenig had seen to that, and now he carefully deployed an army of aristocrats around these common pictures as if dead dukes and duchesses could somehow battle Madison's reason and convince him he was buying masterpieces.

Finally it ended, the six paintings explained into greatness. Bliss no longer slept, but sat alertly on the edge of his chair, eyes wide, and when the Professor bowed, fatigued and trembling, he clapped his great fluke-like hands as if Koenig had given the cue. Rose soon joined in, followed by her father, and from the dimness at the edges of the room, dryly at first, then with increasing enthusiasm, Koenig, the Signora and Clarice began to applaud.

The Professor didn't wait for them to finish but took Rose by the hand and led her from the room. Koenig would divert the others. As for the girl, she was clearly an independent sort. He imagined her in the company of Bliss, prowling the banks of the Arno in search of transvestites, while Madison waited in their hotel suite perusing his Baedeker. Besides, he'd earned her. She was partial payment. Madison's sacrifice.

They crossed the *ingresso* and entered the library. He closed the door and motioned her into the shadows. Then he turned, took off his jacket, folded it carefully over the back of a chair, and removed his trousers, their flared legs sliding easily over his white shoes. When he approached she was ready, like a moth poised against the night sky of the couch.

Finished, he dressed and stepped onto the terrace. It was cool, the dampness settling. The air smelled of cut grass and freshly turned earth. The sun had set, though in the valley the light held on Brunelleschi's dome and the slender, lion-crested tower of the *Palazzo Vecchio*. To the northwest, far down the Arno, spread a russet sheen where the river curved toward Pisa.

His white hands lay on the terrace railing—*pietra serena* carved and laid here in an age when the great Michelangelo walked the streets of the city below. From the north came a distant wail, high and thin, the whistling of a train. He cocked his head, listened. Heard it again. The *Rapido* from Milan. He took a watch of white gold from his vest pocket, snapped open the case, held it high to catch the failing light. On time to the minute. "My God," he murmured, "the man's a genius."

Born and raised in Southern California, Don Meredith migrated to San Francisco in 1960. Within a few years he sailed for Europe, where he lived on a Dalmatian island, then for ten years on a Tuscan farm. Twice a recipient of Fellowships from the National Endowment for the Arts, he is the author of novels, short stories, essays and travel articles. His work has appeared in numerous journals across America, and the University of South Carolina Press will release his book of essays, *Where the Tigers Were*, in 2000. He and his wife Josie make their home on Lamu Island, Kenya.